Dedication

First off, I thank God for the gift to write. My pastor once said a gift is not for you but to share with others. I want to thank my beautiful wife Sparkle Thompson, who has been my greatest supporter. You taught me how to dream again and released the love in my heart.

I thank my Train Service Supervisor and friend Stephen Grant who encouraged me to write through my adversity. I also want to thank and dedicate this book to my children Micaiah, Kyle, Kimberly, Alycia, and Alexis. Always reach for the stars and let nothing stop you.

To my parents Mr. Bernard L. Thompson and Mrs. Jeanette M. Thompson, I thank you for showing me the hidden world of the imagination in books and a special thanks to cousin Brinton Woodall. Thanks for all your help in making this dream a reality. You are a great literary genius. Continue to share your amazing gift with the world.

Excerpt

Suddenly, there was a knock on the front door. Kiera looked through the peephole. It was Mason. "Maybe he forgot something. I'm sure he's not missing me already," she thought to herself.

She started walking towards the door. She unlocked the bolt lock on the door. Slowly she began turning the knob. Suddenly, she stopped. Something was wrong. "He should have a key so, why is he knocking?", she said to herself.

She attempted to lock the door back. BOOM! The door shattered apart. Splinters of wood went flying everywhere...

Mask Of Deception

Chapter 1

Lieutenant Mason Steele's ears rang from the wailing sound of missiles raining overhead. The rest of the platoon had been separated in the ambush. His squad was pinned down and under heavy fire. The enemy was closing in fast.

Less than ten feet away was their Humvee. It seemed to shimmer like a beacon of hope. He looked at the Humvee and then back at his troops. They all had the same idea. However, it seemed as if one of the enemy's soldiers had read their minds.

The soldier stood perched atop a hill with a rocket launcher in hand. Mason knew that he had to do something or they would lose their only means of escape. He slowly began to low crawl to get a better position as his brothers and sisters in arms laid down cover fire. His breathing became shallow as he took aim. Thoughts of his drill Sargent yelling " One shot, one kill " filled his head.

He fired. Almost simultaneously, the rocket launcher fired just as the enemy soldier started to double over. Through the scope of his weapon, Mason could see the bullet had entered through the man's hand and exited his skull.

Mason realized at that moment that he had no time to be proud of his shot. His eyes quickly turned toward the rocket coming their way. He immediately ordered his squad to take cover. It was at that moment that he noticed Specialist Edwards was missing. The rocket screamed overhead. Mason looked towards the Humvee. Specialist Edwards was racing towards it. Within seconds the Humvee was hit, sending shrapnel everywhere. Flames engulfed Edwards.

Mason jumped out of his sleep. He was drenched in sweat. His skin felt cold and clammy. He looked around as he tried to figure out exactly where he was. He could hear the almost deafening sound of his heart pounding in his chest.

As his eyes adjusted to the darkness of the room, he started to make out the furniture. He was in his high rise apartment in New York City. He couldn't shake the thoughts of Specialist Edward's death. Out of the corner of his eye, Mason could see the green glow of his alarm clock illuminating the corner of the room.

It was three o'clock in the morning. Lately these nightmares have been known to keep him up all night. He needed to find something to occupy his mind. Mason stared into the darkness, allowing his eyes a chance to adjust. Once they adjusted, he scanned the room. His gaze fell on the perfect distraction...his weight bench.

He swung his feet over to the side of the bed. The sheets fell off of him as he stood, revealing his nakedness. Mason reached over and turned on the lamp. He then walked toward the linen closet and retrieved a towel. As he closed the closet door, he caught sight of himself in the mirror.

Mason stood at six foot three inches. He weighed two hundred and forty pounds. With merely two percent body fat, he was a very intimidating figure. Mason had a low Caesar style haircut, almost sleepy like brooding hazel green eyes, a rich dark chocolate complexion and dimples, if you could ever catch him smiling. If you asked him though, his best feature was his abs. A person could literally wash clothes on them.

After looking at himself for a few minutes, Mason started his workout. He started with a hundred pushups, crunches, flutter kicks, and some cardio. An hour later, he began lifting weights. He definitely needed this in order to get his mind off things.

The heat became stifling. His body was drenched in sweat. Streaming down his face, his eyes stung as the sweat dripped into his eyes. Mason desperately needed a drink. He placed the weights back on the rack and walked to the small refrigerator in the corner of the room. He reached in and pulled out a nice ice cold bottle of water.

Opening it, he poured some of it on his head before guzzling down the rest. He looked over towards the waste basket and took aim. He attempted to throw the bottle across the the room and into the garbage. Instead the bottle sailed across the room and landed behind the wastebasket. Mason laughed at himself. He definitely was no Michael Jordan.

Grabbing a second bottle of water, Mason slammed the refrigerator door. He sauntered towards the waste basket. Reaching behind it, he took hold of the empty bottle. Laughing at himself, Mason flipped it in the trash. Basketball was never his sport.

Mason stood there, looking out the window. The day was starting out just like any other day in this insane city...cold, dark and empty. He continued to look out the window. The people began scurrying through the streets. They looked like roaches or ants searching for food. As crowded as this city was, a person could easily get lost. This was a place where even amongst a sea of millions a person could feel small and alone.

There was a time when Mason could look from his window and see the marvel that was the original Twin Towers against the skyline. The new towers was built to prove they would not be defeated. A 9/11 museum was also erected so they would never forget. He still remembered that day as if it yesterday. It was a day that truly changed his life. It was the day when the nightmares and the long sleepless nights began.

Mason was a Special Agent working for the New York City Police Department. He had just began his shift when the call came over the six wire. A plane had just crashed into one of the Twin Tower buildings. His mouth dropped open in horror. A multitude of questions ran through his mind. Suddenly, the call of another plane hitting the other Tower came over the six wire. Agents, officers, EMS, and firefighters rushed to the scene. Each of them eager to offer their assistance.

The top floors of both buildings were engulfed in flames. The smoke a dark dense cloud blanketing the sky. The streets of Manhattan were covered in ash. The air was so thick and polluted that many New Yorkers suffered respiratory problems throughout the years that followed. Twisted metal, glass and the bodies of individuals who jumped to escape the flames came plummeting down. Everyone on the ground scattered to keep from getting hit.

The unrelenting screams and the rancid smell of thousands upon thousands of charred remains filled the air. The thought of it still fueled his rage. Suddenly the building imploded, trapping some of his closest friends. Mason had wanted revenge that day. He didn't need a museum to remember. He lived it and would never forget.

Ray J's song "One Wish" suddenly blared from the radio. It startled Mason from his trance. It seems he had just survived another sleepless night. Since he no longer slept, the alarm was merely his daily workout reminder. Mason walked over to the nightstand and lowered the sound. While there he caught the reflection of her window in the mirror.

Chapter 2

Mason didn't exactly know who she was. He remembered her bumping into him like it was yesterday. It was however, in fact, a few months ago. She stood about five foot seven maybe five foot eight inches tall. Her hair draped well past her shoulders.

Her eyes were a beautiful honey brown hue. Anybody who looked into them would easily catch the light dancing in them. The swell of her supple breasts, small waist, southern girl cobra like hips, statuesque legs, high cheekbones and firm butt had him hypnotized.

As he neared the window, he could make out her figure lying across the bed. A small lamp illuminated her room. She rolled over and kicked the covers off of her. She appeared to be naked. Mason reached for his binoculars and raised them to his eyes. His manhood sprang to life at the realization that she actually was.

Mason continued to watch in awe as she began caressing her breasts. She pulled on her nipples and rolled them between her fingers. When her nipples were hard she raised each breast to her lips. Her tongue circled each nipple. All he could think of was those chocolate chip like nipples in his mouth.

Her fingers glided across her body, igniting a fire inside of him. Finally her fingers reached her clit. She began rubbing it in a circular motion. The whole time she continued pinching, pulling, caressing and licking her breasts. He knew deep down inside that he probably shouldn't be watching but he couldn't turn away. Suddenly she stopped.

She rolled over and reached into her nightstand drawer. After a few seconds of rummaging, she seemed to have found exactly what she was searching for. Leaving the drawer open, she pulled out a burgundy silk pouch. Mason watched impatiently. He wanted desperately to know what was inside the pouch.

His question was soon answered. She untied the drawstrings and turned it over. He was shocked yet again. An almost monstrous looking vibrator tumbled out. She laid the pouch down alongside her. A devilish smile appeared on her face as she raised the vibrator in the air. It felt like she wanted him to see.

She twist it in her hands. The beast came to life. It was huge. Mason stood in awe, wondering if he could even measure up. From what he could see it was decorated with studs and lights. It had a rotating head and something to stimulate her clit.

Mason felt as if he was invading her privacy. He wanted to turn and walk away but he kept watching. She turned the vibrator off and parted her thighs. Peering through the binoculars, he could see how wet she was. She continued to rub her clit.

She slowly slid the vibrator into her love canal. She winced a bit and stopped. The head of it was barely in. She took a deep breathe before sliding the rest of it inside her. She moved it in deeper and deeper. Each stroke was faster and more deliberate than the last. The shaft glistened with her sweet nectar. Her mouth opened in ecstasy.

Mason could only imagine how wonderful she might sound. He found himself feeling shocked, guilty, jealous and unbelievably turned on. She reached for the base, turning it on once again.

The lights were a blur as it disappeared inside her. Her hips began bucking as the head rotated inside of her. Her body quivered uncontrollably. She was starting to orgasm Her head was thrown back in euphoric pleasure.

Mason was so caught up from watching her, that he didn't realize that his hand had travelled down to his shaft. Precum glistened on its tip. It had been so long since he had even kissed a woman, let alone made love to one. He didn't know what it was but, something was different about this woman.

Mason's strokes quickened, along his shaft. He imagined her touch, her taste, her scent and her kiss. His breathing was becoming shallow. He was about to cum, fantasizing over a woman that he never even spoke to.

She lay in bed with her head turned toward the window. A smile crept across her face. Mason stumbled back, falling over the weight bench. Feeling embarrassed, he was thankful that all he hurt was his pride.

He sat there trying to remain hidden. He tried to crouch down lower, as he watched her get off the bed and walk towards the window. There she stood, a captivating vision of undeniable beauty. Mason laughed at himself. Here he was, a grown man cowering in the dark from a beautiful woman. He felt absolutely stupid.

Mason summed up the courage to take a peek. She had shut her curtains. He quickly scrambled to his feet. He felt like a stalker. Now feeling embarrassed and throbbing, he attempted to continue his workout.

Mason found his attention constantly being averted toward the window. He hoped she would come back. He closed his eyes. The scene played over and over in his head. Since he didn't get to cum his body ached and yearned for attention.

Mason decided to cut his workout short. He couldn't get his mind off of what he just saw. He walked over to the stereo and searched through his Ipod until he got to "The Best Of Marvin Sease". The song " Candy Licker" resonated throughout the apartment. Satisfied, he walked into the bathroom and turned on the shower. He quickly jumped in. The water was ice cold but, the moment it touch his body, Mason felt his body start to relax.

Chapter 3

Mason knew he had to report into work but, for some reason he didn't want to move. After what seemed like hours, he finally willed himself out of the shower. Drying himself off, Mason wrapped the towel around his waist and walked towards the kitchen. He poured himself a bowl of cereal and leaned back to watch the morning news.

From the corner of his eyes, Mason noticed the sun was starting to rise. Rays of light streamed into the apartment. The glare nearly blinded him. As Mason got up to close the blinds, his attention was again averted to his bedroom. He could hear the morning news playing on the television. Supposedly, crime was at the lowest it had been in five years.

Mason could see down the hall, into his bedroom and out the window. He waited a few minutes. Once he was certain that she wasn't there, he turned and walked towards the living room. Grabbing the remote Mason turned to the music channel. "All Cried Out", an old school ballad by Lisa Lisa and The Cult Jam was on. Shaking his head, Mason leaned against the couch and rubbed his temples.

Looking across the room, his gaze fell on his pearl handled, nickel plated Desert Eagle .45 lying on the coffee table. It was a gift from the military when he got out. For years, a lonely emptiness surged inside him. Today was no different. He had felt dead inside. He figured he might as well finish the job.

Walking across the room, Mason reached for his weapon and slowly raised it to his head. Just then a message about an incoming call flashed across the screen. It was programmed to answer automatically. Suddenly, his partner's voice boomed from his surround sound speakers.

"Hey Mason, What's going on ?," his partner asked.

"Nothing much buddy. Why ? What's up ?," Mason questioned in response.

"I got an important case that just came across my desk. When do you think you'll get here ?," he asked Mason.

Mason placed the gun back on the coffee table. When he turned around, a commercial was showing on the television. He pressed a button on his remote. Johnny's face popped up on the screen.

Mason looked over at the clock on the wall. It was different from most clocks because it was in military time. "I should be there in about thirty minutes ," he responded as he went to empty the remaining bit of cereal.

Just as Mason returned into the room, his towel slipped from around his waist. He scrambled to retrieve it. "Jesus Christ man, could you please put some clothes on? ," Johnny shouted.

"Hey!!! First off, I'm in the privacy of my own home. Secondly, you must admit I am one well put together specimen. After all, you are the one sitting here watching as if this was some sort of pay per - view event," Mason said jokingly.

"Hmm, maybe if you were actually getting some, you wouldn't be trying to flash me," Johnny said sarcastically. He laughed and continued. " I mean how long has it been Mason? You know they say it's unhealthy for a man to spend so much time alone. Besides, why on Earth would I want to watch a short show called " Me, Myself and My Hand?," Johnny asked as he pointed and snickered.

"Johnny, you and I both know meeting a woman has never been a problem. You do remember Sheila, don't you?," Mason asked. Deep down he agreed. It had been far to long since he had even dated, let alone been intimate with a woman.

"We both know that was almost three years ago. A man has needs. You are going to make yourself go blind, if you don't get some soon. Besides, after seeing what's under that towel, it's no wonder why there wasn't a second date," Johnny continued to insult his friend.

"Ha, ha, ha Johnny ! Trust from her screams and moans and the way the neighbors knocked on my door, Sheila had absolutely no problem with me rocking her to sleep," Mason replied.

"Whoa, whoa, whoa T.M.I buddy," Johnny chimed in." That is so nasty. You know darn well, that was some need to know information that I for one, definitely, didn't need to know."

Mason laughed so hard he nearly doubled over. It felt so good to laugh. "It is so nice to know "the reaper" can still laugh," Johnny said after Mason recovered from his contagious laughter. Johnny was one of the few people who was allowed to still call him that.

"Give me a few minutes and I'll meet you at the office," Mason informed him. Hearing that name reminded him of the things, he only wished he could forget.

"Mason, you know I would die for Lisa and that child she's carrying. I only pray you find a love so special," Johnny said.

Mason turned away. He didn't want Johnny to see the tears. He knew he had all but given up on love when Milena disappeared. He knew where Johnny was trying to go but he wasn't trying to have that conversation.

"Why are you still on the phone?," Mason asked, never looking back at the screen. "You know I have to finish getting dressed." Mason made sure this time the towel was securely around his waist.

"I was simply wondering why you was holding that gun in your hand when I called?," Johnny asked.

"Dang these new smart televisions," Mason thought to himself. He had hoped Johnny hadn't noticed. He thought up a quick lie. "I was just about to clean it when you called," Mason answered not daring to look up.

"So where are all the cleaning supplies?," Johnny had further questions.

Since Mason had cleaned his weapon there so many times before, while drinking a blue Curacao, Mason was actually prepared for that question. He reached into the cabinet below and pulled out the cleaning supplies. He then placed them on the table. He hoped that would silence Johnny's interrogation.

Johnny shook his head. "Mason, you can try lying to everyone else including yourself. I for one know you better than you know yourself. Besides, nobody ever cleans a gun with a clip inside, the safety off and the cold steel of the gun pressed against his temple. If you're finished playing Russian Roulette with yourself, I would appreciate you getting dressed and heading over here," Johnny ordered, reprimanding Mason at the same time.

"Johnny! Look I told you I was...," Mason shouted before being cut off.

"Look Mason, you can say or concoct whatever story you want but, I know you better than anyone else," Johnny yelled before the call disconnected.

Mason just stood there staring at the screen. He knew Johnny had hung up. Although it was merely minutes, it had felt like hours. He found himself contemplating on what Johnny had said.

Mason had met Johnny years ago, while they were both in high school. Johnny was always a pretty laid back individual. Johnny was a ladies man. He also excelled in sports. Looking at Mason now nobody would guess that back then he was somewhat of a nerd.

They had met one day, when Tre Donovan and his boys were about to beat Mason up. Although, Mason was attempting to hold his own, Tre and his crew pummeled him to the ground. Johnny was the only one that came to his aid.

After that day, they started working out together. He learned of Johnny's amazing love of martial arts and weaponry. He also learned of his interest in the Japanese language and in business. They immediately became friends. Through the years, they had gotten out of so many tough binds together.

When Mason got out of the military, he had nothing and no one. He came home to an empty house. His wife of six years had vanished. The joint bank account they had was empty. He checked with her parents, coworkers, and friends. None of them, seemed eager to talk to him. It was as if they knew something, that he shouldn't.

Mason checked the hospitals and the morgue. Thankfully, she wasn't there. He posted missing persons flyers all over the city. Try as he might, he just couldn't find her. It drove him even further into a state of depression.

Mason found himself unable to eat or sleep. The silence was foreign to him. He found him drinking morning, noon and night. He drank until he would pass out. He would wake up drenched in sweat and trembling.

Mason had been on the verge of going crazy. Anyone standing close could literally smell the alcohol coming through his pores. Even now, Mason could remember the night, he was so drunk, that he got behind the wheel of a car.

He didn't know how Johnny had got there but, he stopped Mason before he could start the engine. He pulled him out of the car, threw him into a shower and back into a gym. The gym was the one place, Mason could work out his anger, his frustration and his fear.

Mason's world had fell apart around him. He hadn't
showered in weeks. It had been months since he had shaved.
He was about to lose his house and he hadn't been able to
find a job since he got out of the Army. Reconnaissance was
all he knew.

Johnny was the one who got him out of his dark abyss, his
own private hell. They worked out twice a day. Johnny took
the money he had once borrowed from Mason and invested it.
They had made millions. Together they rebuilt the city. Soon
after they opened their detective agency.

Mason walked back into his bedroom and headed towards
the closet. He pulled out his charcoal grey suit, white
shirt, charcoal gray, black and white tie and black leather
dress shoes. As he started to get dressed, Mason found
himself looking back towards the window. He couldn't help
but wonder what she was doing.

Chapter 4

In the building across the way, Kiera had just gotten out of the shower. Walking into her bedroom with lotion in hand, she found her attention drawn to the window. She didn't know what had come over her earlier. It was definitely not something had she ever done before. She didn't even know who he was. Whoever he was, she just couldn't shake him from her thoughts.

Kiera could remember the day she had first laid eyes on him. It was three months ago. She had just moved in. She pulled up in a moving truck and didn't know how she was going to get everything upstairs. She grabbed what she could carry and started moving in.

She had been wearing her low cut shorts, a white fitted T-shirt and white sneakers. Cars drove past. Men honked like horny teenage boys. Other men walked down the street whistling and catcalling her. Some of them tried to get her name and number. Some of them even stopped and stared but, nobody volunteered to help. They had made her feel like a sex object that day. At some point, she considered running upstairs and changing into some oversized sweats and a baseball cap.

When Kiera looked up, she see a group of men walking in her direction. She was prepared to hide to avoid more catcalls. They stopped at the building next door. One of them, walked up and asked if she needed assistance. She looked up to see who it was. It was him.

The men stayed and helped her until, she was completely moved in. They even organized her furniture exactly like she wanted it. Before she could even say "thank you", they were all gone.

14

Imagine her amazement when she got in late one night
from work and looked out her window. It had been raining
that night. She rushed in. Her clothes were dripping wet.
Slow jams were playing on the radio. She stripped out of her
clothes that night and hopped in the shower while her
lasagna warmed up in the oven.

After she finished eating, she went to wash dishes. She
saw movement out the corner of her eye. She walked slowly
toward her bedroom as if in a trance. When she looked out
the window there he was. He was working out in the nude. The
sight of him had turned her on.

Kiera wasn't sure if it was the sight of him that night
that sent a hot flash of passion through her body. Then
again, maybe, it was the rain. Something about the rain had
always turned her on. Perhaps, it was a combination of the
two. Whatever it was, she wanted him that night.

From that day forth, she just couldn't shake him from
her mind. She found herself wondering if he was married?
Single? Dating? Employed, if he had kids? Lived with his
parents? Was straight or homosexual? She felt foolish in her
thinking. She had never seen him with anyone but this one
other man.

The guy she saw him with was well built , polite, and
soft spoken. She had to admit the man was very attractive.
Come to think about it, he was also one of the men that
helped, when she moved in.

Kiera hoped her little show had peaked her neighbor's
interest. She had to smile just thinking about it. She
reached into her closet and grabbed her clothes for work.
Once dressed, she looked over at the clock. She was running
late. She grabbed her purse, her keys and left.

Once she locked her apartment door, Kiera headed for
the elevator. She pushed the button and waited. Shortly
after she heard the ding of the arriving elevator. The doors
opened and revealed it was empty.

She walked in and hit the button for the lobby. Thoughts
of this morning's events and watching him touch himself as
he watched her entered her mind. A wicked smile came across
her face. The elevator doors closed behind her.

Chapter 5

Mason looked into the mirror. Not a line out place. Opening his top drawer, Mason took out his Sterling silver diamond encrusted watch with the pearl face. He smiled. He always believed he cleaned up nicely.

Walking into the kitchen, he grabbed his key and headed for the door. He stopped midway. He ran through a list in his head. He wanted to be certain he wasn't leaving anything. Once he was satisfied, Mason set the alarm. As the alarm counted down, he made a mad dash for the door.

Securing it on the outside, he walked to his private elevator. The elevator doors opened and he walked inside. Mason pushed button for the lobby as the doors closed behind him. Mason was distracted. Once again his mind was on the mysterious woman across the way.

He couldn't help but wish it was him taking her to the heights of ecstasy this morning. Suddenly, the doors opened. Mason was a little shocked that he had already arrived in the lobby. Dexter sat behind the desk, talking on the phone.

Mason waved and headed for the door. Looking like a relay runner, Dexter rushed from behind the desk with newspaper in hand. "Good morning Mr. Steele. You look very sharp this morning," Dexter said.

17

A smile appearing as if glued to his face. "Good morning Dex. I do hope all is well," Mason replied.

"It sure is. I just wanted to thank once again, for the job you got me. I just don't know how to repay you," Dexter said.

Dexter was prior military. Unfortunately, he barely received anything as payment for his injury. He could barely take care of himself, let alone his daughter. He was arrested for breaking and entering a pharmacy some years back. He stole medication for himself and diapers and for his then two month old baby girl. Due to that, Dexter was just released from prison a few days ago.

"You can pay me back staying out of trouble. Make sure you kiss that beautiful little lady and tell her I said hello," Mason informed him.

He then walked away before Dexter could say anything else. As soon as Mason stepped outside he saw the sexiest pair of legs ever. He immediately knew it was her. He found himself tempted to run after her.

He was at a loss for words. She was beautiful. Mason walked behind her as if in a trance. The swaying of her cobra hips were hypnotizing. She was every man's dream. Mason didn't dare think he had a chance.

As if she could hear his thoughts, she stopped. Her clothes flowed gently over her shapely frame. She turned around. Mason got nervous and walked towards his car. He could feel her eyes on him. He didn't look back. Instead, he opened the door to his red and black Charger and hopped inside.

Just as he rolled down the windows R. Kelly's " Move Your Body Like A Snake" blared from the radio. Mason instantly thought of how her body moved. Their eyes locked. She licked her lips and smiled. His manhood throbbed. He wanted her

badly but, he was so tired of one night stands. He needed more. He needed something real. She looked away.

Mason revved his engine but she seemed interested in something else. Disappointed, he pulled away from the curb. He got as far as the curb and found himself stuck behind a red light. Mason looked in his rearview mirror. She was looking. Then she disappeared down the subway steps. He thought to himself "Someday Mason someday."

Chapter 6

Mason didn't even know when the light changed. The sounds of people shouting curses and leaning on their horns shook him from his thoughts. When he looked up at the light, it had just turned yellow. Mason sped through just before it turned red. He could just imagine how angry everyone behind him was. It made him laugh.

Ten minutes later, Mason pulled up to a beautiful twelve story brown stone building. He parked his car and walked into the lobby. Once inside, he walked towards the elevator. He pushed the button.

After a few minutes, Mason noticed nothing was moving. He went to push it again and noticed the out of order sign posted on the wall. Mason shook his head. How had he missed that before? He had to get that woman out of his head.

Mason looked to his left and headed in the direction of the stairs. He hated stairs. Time to see if all the cardio he was doing was working. He sighed and took a deep breath. He began running up the stairs, two at a time. After five minutes he saw a sign for the twelfth floor. He barely broke a sweat. He guess it's working.

Once on the twelfth floor, Mason made a left and walked down the hall. There in front of him was his office. Steele and Nightshade Detective Agency was emblazoned on the door. Since, they didn't exactly need the money, they found themselves doing a lot of pro bono work.

Mason peeked inside. Johnny was sitting behind his desk with his back to the door. Mason slowly opened the door and slipped inside. He slowly tried closing the door back in hopes that Johnny wouldn't hear it. A throwing star flew past his head and got lodged into the wall in front of him. Mason whirled around. Johnny had stood up and was looking directly at him.

"It's about time you showed up. I hope you know that I am still upset about what I saw earlier but we have to meet up with Col. Blake. Trust me when I say, we will talk about it later," Johnny said with a look of disappointment on his face.

"Yes mom," Mason said jokingly. His words were instantly cut off by the angry scowl on Johnny's face.

"So did the Colonel say what this was in reference to?," Mason asked, quickly trying to change the subject.

Johnny's fist were balled up. He punched the wall next to him, leaving a hole in it. Johnny was pissed. Johnny was the closest thing Mason had to family. He was more like a brother to Mason than a friend. Mason knew the conversation was far from over.

After a deep sigh Johnny finally answered, "He didn't exactly say but, I'm sure we both know what it's in reference to." Johnny then grabbed his jacket and headed out the office. Mason followed suit. Johnny walked towards the elevator. He had a sense of urgency in each step.

"The elevator is out," Mason shouted as he headed towards the stairs.

Johnny reached in his pocket and pulled out a key. He stuck it in the elevator keyhole on the wall. Suddenly, Mason heard the clanging of the wheels coming to life. He looked up and saw the numbers rapidly moving. Mason had to laugh as he shut the door leading to the stairs and headed back towards the elevator.

"Really Johnny?," Mason asked with a dumbfounded look on his face.

"Yeah fatso. I figured after that foolishness this morning, I would make you suffer a bit," he replied.

"But how...?", Mason started to question how he pulled it off before, he remembered Johnny could hack into anything. He was almost certain Johnny had hacked the security cameras ,watched him enter the building and shut down the elevator. Now he was left wondering how Johnny got the key and the Out Of Order sign.

They both got into the elevator. The doors closed behind them. Neither of them said a word as the elevator began its descent. As soon as, they stepped out of the elevator and into the lobby, it started raining. No one had an umbrella.

" What's the best way to get there?", "Should we drive or take the train?," Johnny asked.

Although Mason wanted to drive, he knew that wasn't the best option. "Johnny, we both know crazy traffic can be on Linden Boulevard. Then we would have to take into account, how slow they drive when it's raining. Mason reminded him.

" Drive!!!," they both exclaimed simultaneously. "Jinx!!!," they yelled and began laughing as they remembered their old childhood game.

They pulled their jackets down snug around their heads and stepped outside. The rain was coming down hard. Mason and Johnny took off running. Seeming so far away, the train station loomed in the distance.

Chapter 7

Drenched, they finally made it to the train station. A train was screeching out of the station. We paid our fare and walked through the turnstile. The passengers looked like wild cattle stampeding past them.

Once they were on the platform, they noticed it was almost empty. A young, fit, homeless man dug through the trash bins. The man was wearing old, tattered and dirty clothes. Mason noticed his tattoo. It was the exact same one Mason had.

The man seemed a bit jittery and defensive. Mason approached him slowly. " Excuse me sir, Are you hungry?," Mason asked, realizing as drenched as he was, he looked homeless as well.

The man looked Mason up and down. A bit hesitant, the man finally spoke, " I haven't eaten in days."

Mason felt the anger boiling inside him. Here was a man who fought for his country and now the man is out on the streets, tossed away like yesterday's garbage. Mason reached in his pocket and retrieved his wallet. He took out a stack of money and a card. Mason stretched his hand out to offer its contents to the homeless man. Instead of taking it, the man shook his head and backed away.

"What's wrong?," Mason asked looking somewhat bewildered.

"I-I-I j-j-just don't take any handouts," he stammered.

" I understand Mr. ?," Mason said.

" My name is Richard Eason and I don't take handouts sir," the man answered back.

"My name is Mason Steele and if you are willing to work, then take it as an advance. Also, if you go to the address on this card you will find a fully furnished apartment. It's yours if you want it," Mason informed him.

"Look sir, no offense but I am not trying to sell drugs for anyone. I also am not trying to go back to sleeping on some rickety old cot in some shelter. I had enough of that in the military. Thanks but no thanks," the man screamed, shoving the money and card into Mason's chest.

Mason rolled up his sleeve. For the first time, the man saw Mason's tattoo. A confused look appeared on the man's face. "What is your name again?," the man asked.

"My name is Mason Steele but my friends just call me Mason", Mason replied as he extended his hand once more.

" Lieutenant Steele?," the man asked as he stood at attention.

"No need for that Richard. I do hope I can call you Richard. I also hope that you will accept my offer," Mason said as he tried placing the card and money in Richard's hand.

"Why are you doing this Mr. Steele?," Richard asked. "You don't even know me".

"After what I went through, I swore to always look after those less fortunate than I. I also vowed to have my fellow veterans and soldiers backs. I am my brother's keeper", Mason told him.

Richard took the money out of Mason's hand. He looked at it for a few minutes. When he realized Mason had given him well over a thousand dollars, his eyes began to tear up. " I can't accept this Mr. Steele. It's way too much money," Richard said. Tears streamed down his face.

"You deserve it. Do me a favor and see it as a thank you. A thank you for all you sacrificed and may have lost being on the front line", Mason replied.

"Lieutenant Steele, I know who you are and everything you did out there. It is I that should be thankful. You know what it was like out there. My whole life changed. I was eighteen years old and fresh out of high school. I saw things nobody should ever see. The nightmares are so bad that I can't sleep at night. I lost people I cared about," Richard said crying.

"Trust me Richard when I say, I left there with my own demons. I always told myself, that if I am ever in a position to help a fellow soldier I would. When I came back, I had nothing. A good friend or more like a brother, helped me to get back on my feet. Today is the start of a way back for you. Take it", Mason said, trying to fight back his own tears.

"Thank you Lieutenant Steele," Richard said as he finally accepted the card and money.

"I need you to do one more favor for me Richard," Mason said with a smile.

"What do you need?," Richard asked. There was now a smile on his face and a sense of hope.

"First stop calling me Lieutenant Steele. My friends call me Mason. Secondly, go out and buy yourself some clothes. Then go over to Geraldo's and tell him I sent you. He will make sure you get something to eat," Mason said, smiling back.

"Wow Lieutenant.... er I mean Mason are you serious? This truly can't be happening," Richard said with a shocked look on his face.

"If you are truly serious about getting back on your feet then, this is definitely happening," Mason replied.

"Mason, I could kiss you", Richard exclaimed.

"If you do I might punch you," Mason said and laughed. "How about a hug and a handshake? That is, if you don't mind the wet clothes."

Richard stepped forward but was a bit apprehensive at first. He was worried that Mason would be turned off by his smell. Sensing that, Mason walked up and gave Richard a hearty hug and shook his hand. Richard then turned and walked off. There was a renewed, robust vigor in his step.

Mason walked over to where Johnny was standing. Johnny had a big grin on his face as he looked at Mason. "Why are you smiling, old friend?," Mason asked, already knowing the answer.

"I'm smiling because you know you're a big softie. That's the very reason that Lisa and I made you our kids godfather." Johnny said.

Suddenly Mason heard a shrill bird call. Without hesitation, Mason's body stiffened up. His mind switched into a different mode. Johnny looked at Mason and knew there was about to be some trouble.

Chapter 8

Mason stood there a bit bewildered at first. Not too many people knew the signal. They used it to warn each other of approaching danger, when he was in the military. Almost instinctively, Mason signaled back. Suddenly, Mason knew who was signaling him. It was Richard.

In the distance, Mason and Johnny could hear trash cans being overturned. They saw the sparks and smelled the smoke of some of them crashing onto the tracks. The sound was getting closer. They didn't know who was coming but they knew whoever it was, was here to start some trouble and there was quite a few of them. An elderly couple had just came downstairs to wait for the train. Besides, that nobody else was around.

Just then, they heard the elderly woman's frail scream. One of the guys had snatched the woman's purse and shoved her to the ground. The rest of the men stood around laughing. She lie there motionless. Her husband saw what happened and attempted to stand up, only to get pushed back down. The men started to kick his wife.

The elderly man grabbed his cane. One of the men stood there taunting him and laughing. Suddenly, the elderly man struck the man on the side of his head with his cane. Now embarrassed, the man grabbed the elderly man by the collar and began to repeatedly punch him in his face.

The rest of the thugs cheered him on. They were proud of this. Mason and Johnny were angry. As they approached the thugs, Mason and Johnny attempted to assess the situation.

"Why don't you respect your elders and learn to pick on someone your own size?", Johnny shouted.

Mason and Johnny both stood at six foot three inches tall. The gang leader still had about four inches over them. Laughing, he finally let go of the elderly man. The man collapsed in a pool of his own blood. Groaning and sore, the man crawled over to his wife. She still lay there motionless. He used his own body to shield hers.

The gang leader stepped towards Mason and Johnny. The rest of the thugs followed, surrounding them. Once all of them were distracted Richard ran to the aide of the elderly couple. He got the couple onto their feet and out of harm's way. He then came back, wanting to help. Mason and Johnny signaled for him to leave.

"You should have minded your own business," the leader yelled.

He snapped his fingers. The rest of the gang began to charge Mason and Johnny. One of them grabbed a trash can and hurled it in their direction. They both ducked. The trash can struck one of the other members in the head. The guy fell back unconscious, blood dripped from his head. Mason and Johnny laughed.

Mason and Johnny soon realized that only angered the leader. He began swinging wildly at Mason and Johnny. He hit Mason first. Mason fell to the ground. The gang leader then whirled around and caught Johnny with an elbow. Johnny fell to his knee.

Mason and Johnny knew the rest of the gang would turn and run, if they took down the leader. They would have to team together to do that. They shook their heads as they tried to get their bearings and got to their feet.

"Hey little Mason Squeal, No matter how much you work out you will always be a little man to me ," the leader said chuckling.

Mason hadn't been called that since high school. The laugh suddenly sounded eerily familiar. It was a mocking, cocky laugh that sent chills up your spine. A laugh nobody would ever forget. "It can't be him," Mason said to himself. As Mason scrambled to his feet, he looked into the leader's eyes. It was him. It was Tre Donovan. He went by the name T-Rex.

Mason found himself laughing. He got to his seat and brushed himself off. He looked over at Johnny. Johnny was also back on his feet. Mason used to be terrified of this guy. Now he just felt sorry for Tre.

"Why are you laughing?," Tre asked angrily.

"Well that's an easy question. Mason finally realized why they call you T-Rex. Sure just like a T-Rex you are big, strong and scary looking. However, just like a T-Rex , you have a pea sized brain," Mason said, still laughing.

Talking about Tre was something no one ever did. Tre was the leader of the notorious Hell Raisers. He was also the biggest drug dealer and pimp on the East Coast. If it was illegal, he did it. He had been accused of more than half the murders in the city.

"Get them," Tre ordered. They could almost see the steam rising off of him. He shook uncontrollably in anger. He was like a tea pot about to blow his whistle. Johnny looked at Mason. He didn't agree with Mason's decision to mock Tre.

Tre's gang charged them. Mason and Johnny pulled out their batons. One of the men grabbed Mason from behind. Two of his cohorts took turns repeatedly punching Mason in his face and ribs. Mason looked for help but Johnny was busy with three other adversaries. Tre stood back watching and licking his chops. He was a ravenous lion awaiting the kill.

Mason tried to wiggle free to no avail. A minutes later, Mason had an idea. He just hoped it would work. Mason moved forward, taking the guy off his feet.

When the guy holding Mason attempted to lean back and
regain his footing, Mason rammed his head back. Mason head
hit him in his mouth. That forced him to release his hold.
He stood there wincing in pain.

Mason turned around to face him. The gang member was
bleeding profusely from his mouth. At first, he cursed
Mason. Then the guy muttered something about his teeth. When
Mason looked down between them, two of the guy's teeth were
lying on the platform.

Despite the pain he was in, the man attempted to grab
Mason once more. Mason grabbed the back of the man's head
and pulled it down. At the same time Mason raised his leg.
He rammed his knee into the guy's face. The guy fell back
onto the platform. His face was bleeding profusely as he lie
unconscious.

Mason turned back to face the other two men. They both
now stood with knives in their hands. Mason looked down to
see his hands were empty. In all the confusion, Mason
managed to drop his baton. Mason looked around for it.
Finally he saw it. The baton lie on the platform beside the
man he had just knocked out.

Mason turned back in the nick of time. The other two
were closing in. Their knives sliced through the air. Mason
stepped back, rolled and grabbed the baton. Just as one of
them swung their knife close to his face.

Mason swung the baton. It cracked the man on his
wrist. Judging by the way it bent, Mason knew he had broke
it. Now defenseless the man fell to the ground, writhing in
pain.

Mason side stepped the last one. He then placed the
man in a headlock. The man dropped the knife as he struggled
to gasp for air. Mason tightened his grip. The man's arms
fell to his side. Mason released his grip and watched the
man crumble to the platform.

Mason looked around. He felt proud of the short work, he had made of them. That was until he turned and looked at Johnny. Johnny was already leaning against a pillar smiling. His adversaries lay sprawled out, bloody and ached.

Suddenly, we heard an almost animalistic growl. They had forgotten about Tre. He knew they would have to celebrate later. They stood side by side as they prepared to face Tre.

Tre charged them. He moved with reckless abandon. He grabbed Johnny and slammed him to the ground. Mason swung at Tre with his baton. Tre seemed unfazed. With unparalleled quickness, Tre grabbed Mason by his throat and pushed him backwards towards the track.

Mason found himself losing consciousness. His knees were buckling. Nothing Mason did fazed Tre. Tre dangled Mason over the tracks. Mason thought he was good as dead. Suddenly, Johnny struck him behind his knee with the baton. Tre loosened his grip and fell to one knee. Mason pulled away. Still gasping for air, Mason crawled away from the platform edge. Still coughing, he stood to his feet.

Tre stood up limping. He charged at Johnny. Johnny turned and struck him across the bridge of the nose. Tre's eyes watered. Mason and Johnny had to move quickly. They both kicked him and sent him reeling back. Tre stood teetering on the edge.

He struggled desperately to regain his balance. Suddenly, they heard the announcement of an oncoming train. Tre panicked. Still in pain, his knee gave out. His body collapsed to the tracks below.

From the distance, they could feel a cool rush of air. They couldn't see the train but knew it was approaching fast. Tre screamed for help. His gang members raced to his aide. The train came around the curve. It's lights got closer by the second. The gang struggled to pull Tre up.

The train operator began blowing the train horn. Tre's legs were still dangling over the edge. The operator grabbed the brakes. Tre's gang made a last ditch effort to pull him away from the edge. It worked. The train screeched completely in the station.

The train doors opened and both Mason and Johnny got on. As they looked back, Mason pointed. Johnny saw it too. Apparently, Tre had peed his pants from the fear of almost being ran over.

Tre quickly recovered from his fear when he saw them laugh. He shoved his men out the way and charged towards them. The train doors closed in his face. He immediately started cursing and throwing things.

Chapter 9

Mason and Johnny stood ready in case the doors reopened. Neither of them wanted to go another with Tre, but they wouldn't get caught off guard. The train started moving. Mason had a feeling that, that wouldn't be the last they saw of him.

Mason straightened out his clothes and sat down. Johnny stood leaning against the train's doors. Neither of them said a word to one another. Thirty minutes later, the train pulled into Gaskins Avenue station. They had to push through a crowd in order to exit the train.

Once outside, they noticed the rain had stopped. Peddlers stood outside of the station. They were selling everything from purses to fruit and from laundry detergent to cigarettes. Life was a hustle.

Mason and Johnny walked five blocks before they reached a building with a fire breathing dragon in front of it. Mason opened the door. A sign welcoming them to the Red Dragon Lounge illuminated the doorway. The inside was beautiful. The walls were red with gold trim. Tea candles flickered at each table. A huge red dragon statue sat in the center of the room. Music played in the background.

"About time you got here," Mason heard an all too familiar voice say from somewhere inside the lounge.

Mason looked around until his gaze fell on a short, somewhat stout, older, light skin gentleman. It was Colonel Blake. "Well, well, well you old dog. How have you been Colonel?," Mason asked.

"Look little brother, you need to cut that Colonel crap out," he replied. Mason found himself laughing. Colonel Blake's booming voice didn't quite fit his somewhat diminutive stature.

"Alright James, how have you and the Mrs. been doing?," Mason questioned.

"She's good Mason. She actually told me to ask you, what rock have you been hiding under? We haven't seen you in a long time," he replied.

Colonel Blake was Mason's mentor in the military. If it wasn't for him, Mason doubted he would have made it. Him and his wife were the parents Mason never had. Mason walked over and gave him a hug.

"I've just been going through some things. Tell her I will try to stop by real soon," Mason told him. For some reason, Mason felt extremely bad for not seeing them in such a long time.

"I'll definitely do that. The government loves the prototype you two developed. They want to test it in the field soon," Colonel Blake informed them. He could barely hold back his excitement.

"That's great James. It could mean that no soldier will ever go missing in action again," Mason said.

"However....," Colonel Blake said. Mason looked in his eyes. He could see the Colonel was trying to mask his concern. "We recently got word that there are others that know about Keeper. They hope to steal it and sell it to our enemies."

"James, I won't let them. We can't let them get their hands on " Keeper," Mason said already knowing the damage it could cause.

"We won't Mason. I need you to hold on to it. Hide it in a safe place. We'll meet in a few weeks to run those field tests and have a little family dinner," Blake said trying to comfort his friend.

"I can definitely do that James. Thanks for the heads up. Be careful," Mason said as he hugged him.

"I will. Please do the same. Be careful who you talk to. Linda and I love you," Blake informed him.

"I love you both as well," Mason said. Tears streamed down his face. Mason was scared to release the hold he had on Blake.

Mason and Johnny said their goodbyes to Colonel Blake. They then turned and walked back towards the door. Mason turned to look back. Colonel Blake stood there smiling and waving. He took his role of being undercover seriously. Mason felt an uneasy feeling in his gut. He forced himself to smile, waved and then left.

"You okay Mason?," Johnny asked. Mason wondered if he could see something was bothering him.

"Yeah Johnny!! I just got this strange feeling. I'm sure it's nothing though," Mason told him. He wasn't quite sure if he even believed that though.

They both walked towards the subway in silence. Mason couldn't shake the feeling. As he walked, Mason found himself doing something he hadn't done in years. Mason prayed.

As they neared the station, they felt a rumble beneath their feet. They both remembered what happened the last time they missed the train. Mason and Johnny looked at each other. Without saying anything they raced for the train.

Chapter 10

After Mason and his partner left, Colonel Blake just
stood there. Mason was like a son to him and he missed him.
He hadn't spoken to him since Mason's wife left. It had been
even longer since he had saw him.

Colonel Blake looked around the lounge. It was
beautiful. "Maybe when I retire, I will own one of my own,"
he thought to himself. Suddenly , his phone rang.

"Sir, It's Sergeant Reese. We are on our way to your
location. Are you almost done?," the voice on the phone
asked.

"I am," Colonel Blake replied. "I will be outside
waiting.

Colonel Blake went into the back and thanked the
manager. He then, went into the locker. He changed out of
the Red Dragon uniform and back into his street clothes.
Blake looked down at his watch. Sergeant Reese should be
outside soon. Checking to make sure he had everything, Blake
headed towards the rear exit of the building.

Ten minutes later, a van pulled up in front of him.
This wasn't his car but he decided to get in once he saw
Sargent Reese sitting behind the steering wheel. Reese had
his cap down, concealing his eyes.
" Sir, are you ready to go?," Reese asked.

"Yes I am Sergeant. By the way where is my car?," Blake
asked.

"Sir, your car had a bit of a transmission problem. I
dropped it off at the mechanic and borrowed this from the
motor pool," Reese quickly responded.

Blake reached for the door handle. Out of the corner of his eye he saw movement. Blake reached for his side arm. It was a gift from Mason. He barely gripped the handle before he felt a sharp piercing pain. He looked down. Blood stained his shirt.

Blake looked over at Reese who seemed to have an evil yet confused look on his face. It was at that moment, Colonel Blake knew. The man in front of him wasn't Sergeant Reese. Sure he completely looked and sounded like him but, it wasn't him. Blake tried to turn and run for help. He was losing blood fast.

"Why?," Blake questioned the man, he once believed was Sergeant Reese. He never got his answer. Seconds later Blake lay dead, in a pool of his own blood.

The man pulled off his mask. He then looked at the intimidating figure that stood over Colonel Blake's lifeless body.

"Did I tell you to kill him?," the man asked screaming.

"No sir! I am sorry but, he was reaching for his gun. Besides, any friend of Mason Steele is an enemy of mine. I am more than that with Blake dead Mason will come looking for his killer," Tre said laughing.
"We needed information on the Keeper project and its whereabouts. For your sake you better hope you're right," the man replied.

Tre ran the streets. The mere mention of his name made most men cower. Tre also had some cops on his payroll so he didn't fear to many men. Chameleon was different. Tre had seen the things this man had done to anyone that failed him. He knew he didn't want to be next.

"Get him in the van," Chameleon ordered.

Tre did as he was ordered. He threw Colonel Blake's lifeless body over his shoulder. Opening the van door, he dumped the corpse inside. Thirty minutes later, they arrived at Far Rockaway beach. Tre stepped out of the van and looked around.

Satisfied that no one was around Tre reached inside the back of the van. Grabbing two cement blocks and some rope, he bounded the legs of the corpse. He looked around once more. Certain the coast was clear, Tre dragged Blake's body out of the van. Hoisting the lifeless body on his shoulder,

Tre walked to the water. He threw the body into the ocean and watched it sink to the murky depths below. When Tre returned he learned that Chameleon had switched seats. Tre got behind the wheel. He looked over to see Chameleon staring at the crashing waves. Tre started the engine and they disappeared into the night.

Chapter 11

Mason couldn't shake the strange feeling. He was quiet the whole ride back to the office. As soon as he stepped out of the subway station, Mason was on his phone trying to reach Colonel Blake. Try as he might, the calks went straight to voicemail.

Johnny instantly knew something was troubling his best friend. They had been friends for far too long for him not to. He searched his mind for something to say to comfort him. Unfortunately, Johnny didn't even know what to say. He didn't even know what was wrong.

Just then Mason's phone rang. He looked down at it. It was an unknown number. Normally, Mason didn't answer calls from an unknown number. This time he did.

"Hello! Hello!!," the voice on the other end kept saying. It was a female's voice. It sounded familiar but Mason had trouble placing it.

"Hello?," Mason responded as he struggled to place the voice.

"Mason?", "It's me Linda," she said. It took a minute for the name to register. "Linda! Linda!," he thought to himself. Finally it came to him. Linda? It was Colonel Blake's wife.

"Hey Miss Linda, how have you been?," Mason asked.

"I'm doing well Mason. How are you?," she asked.

"I'm okay. I have been trying to reach James but my calls keep going to voicemail", he told her.

"Yeah I know. He called me a little while ago. He said he had a meeting to go to. He also said you sounded a bit worried and asked me to check on you. James will be heading out of town later to work on some project you two were discussing," she informed him.

"Oh ok! Do you know when he'll be back. I've got this weird feeling and I won't be comfortable until I speak to him," he told her.

"Well I assure you that he sounded fine. I think he said he would gone for a month. I will be so happy when he gets home. I worry about and miss him so much when he's away. By the way, I do hope you come visit soon. We miss seeing you," Linda said. You could hear the love she felt for him. She often tried to hide how much her husband being away bothered her.

"I miss you both as well Linda. I'll make sure that I stop by soon," Mason told her.
"Well I have some errands to run. It's been great talking to you. We definitely must do this again.

"I love you," Linda said.

"Okay Linda, I'll talk to you later. I love you too. Take care", Mason replied. She hung up. Mason felt a little more at ease but still couldn't shake the strange feeling.

Meanwhile in Pennsylvania, Linda sat back shaking. She had done exactly as instructed. As the men searched through her house, she didn't know what to do. She thought about running but she knew she wouldn't get far.

A big behemoth of a man guarded the front door. Another man that she had mistaken for her husband sat a few inches behind her. She wanted desperately to say something to Mason. A gun with a silencer was pressed against her head.

Linda couldn't stop shaking. Where was James? What was happening? Why was it happening? These questions and many more kept running through her head.

"Where is it Mrs. Blake?", James' doppelganger asked.

"What? What are y-y-you talking about?," she asked nervously.

"Your husband was working on a Top Secret project for a prototype that can locate any military personnel anywhere in the world whether stateside overseas. We want it ma'am," James's lookalike demanded as he sat in the shadows.

"I don't know what you're even talking about. He doesn't tell me anything that goes on in the military. Please don't kill me. Just go. I promise I won't tell anyone," Linda said. Her voice quivering as she spoke.

"I believe you. I know you won't tell anyone," the man said. His gaze fell on the huge man guarding the door. As if on key Tre lumbered over to Mrs. Blake. His huge hand completely covered her mouth. Seconds later, her body went limp in his arms. Her eyes rolled to the back of her head. She was gone.

Tre smiled and watched as her body crashed to the floor. He seemed to take pleasure in taking someone's life. They then packed her a suitcase and grabbed her purse and identification. Wrapping her body up in a rug, they dumped her corpse into an awaiting van. The other men remained to scrub the house clean, as the van drove away.

Tre and Chameleon drove out to the river. Tre knew the routine. He bound Mrs. Blake's legs to the cement blocks, just like he had done her husband's. He was prepared to throw her body into the river, when Chameleon appeared at his side. Chameleon placed his hands on her face, shutting her eyelids.

"May you and your husband find joy, comfort, love and each other in the afterlife", Chameleon prayed before turning and walking a way. Tre then pushed Mrs. Blake's body into the river. A single tear fell from Chameleon's eye, as her body disappeared beneath the murky dark water below.

Chapter 12

Mrs. Lisa Nightshade had just gotten to the Whalen Medical Center. She looked nervously at her watch. She was forty five minutes late for her appointment. She wished Johnny was there. She hated that he had to go into work today.

Her feet were swollen. Her back ached. Some days she couldn't hold down her food. Lisa rubbed her stomach. It was hard for her to believe there was a life growing inside of there.

As the elevator chimed through each floor, her excitement rose. For months, she was wondering whether they were having a boy or a girl. Today she finds out. Finally the elevator stopped on the floor she needed. The doors slid open slowly. The sign in front of her pointed in the direction of Labor and Delivery. The thought of it made Lisa nervous.

Lisa walked up to the front desk to check in. Her hands were shaking. A beautiful woman with a southern accent instructed her to sit down and she would be with her momentarily. Lisa did as instructed. A few minutes later, the nurse called her into a room.

"Good morning ma'am. How can I help you today?," The nurse politely asked.

Lisa could tell that the nurse loved her job. She was so polite and well spoken. She was also stunningly beautiful. This was the type of woman she thought Mason should be with.

"Well, I am here today to learn the sex of the baby I'm having," Lisa told her. Excitement was welling up inside of her.

The nurse checked her vitals first. Everything was fine. The nurse then had her lay down on the table. She rubbed gel on Lisa's stomach and turned on the sonogram machine.

The nurse took her time, carefully searching for a little. This was truly one of the great joys about her job. She loved babies and their innocence. She heard a heartbeat. She smiled and looked at the screen.

"Well Mrs. Nightshade I've got some news for you?," the nurse said.

"What is it? Is everything alright? ," Lisa asked nervously.

The nurse easily picked up on her concerns. She immediately attempted to put Mrs. Nightshade at ease. "No, no ma'am. It's nothing bad let me assure you," the nurse said now a little excited herself.

"Are you sure?," Lisa asked.

"Oh trust me, Mrs. Nightshade. You are pregnant with twins. You are having a boy and a girl," the nurse said as she held Lisa's hand.

Lisa couldn't believe it. Her and Johnny had been trying for a while to conceive. When she found out she was pregnant, she couldn't help but fall to her knees and thank God. When she told Johnny that she was pregnant, he was overjoyed.

She recalled how they went back and forth, trying to guess the sex of the baby. They eventually came to the realization that they would both be happy, just as long as the baby was healthy. Now she was hearing this.

"Are you sure? When I came here before they never saw twins," Lisa asked barely able to contain her excitement.

44

"Yes ma'am I am. One was hiding directly behind the other. Look here, I'll show you," the nurse replied and proceeded to show her.

Lisa was amazed. She saw the babies kicking. Lisa smiled. The babies appeared to be sucking their thumbs. She heard their tiny little heartbeats. She giggled with joy. Yes, she was having twins. Lisa started to cry.

"Are you alright Mrs. Nightshade?," the nurse asked.

"Oh yes, this is wonderful news. By the way, my name is Lisa. You make me feel so old calling ma'am and Mrs. Nightshade," Lisa told her.

"Glad to hear that Lisa," the nurse replied.

"Can I ask exactly where you're from?," Lisa asked.

"Well, I just moved here from Tennessee a few months ago," the nurse answered.

"Did you move out here with your husband? Kids? Family?," Lisa inquired. She couldn't help but feel this nurse would be a perfect match for Johnny's partner.

"I'm. I don't have any kids. I don't have any family or friends out here. By the way, would you know of a good church I can go to?," the nurse replied.

"Great!," Lisa thought to herself. She liked the fact the nurse was a spiritual woman. Mason needed someone positive, supportive, intelligent, attractive and spiritual.

"Well I go to a wonderful church, The Faith and Fellowship Christian Center. Pastor Shelton P. Boyce is the senior pastor. If you aren't too busy Sunday perhaps, you and your boyfriend can join me and my husband," Lisa said, still hoping to find out one important piece of information.

"That would be wonderful. I just so happen to be off this weekend. Unfortunately, though it will just be me. I'm single and haven't found Mr. Right just yet," the nurse told her. Lisa smiled.

"Jackpot! She's single," Lisa said to herself. They exchanged cards and said their goodbyes. Lisa then headed to the front desk to schedule her next appointment. Once finished Lisa headed to the elevator.

As soon as she got inside, Lisa looked at the business card she held tightly in her grasp. It read Ms. Kiera Williams Registered Nurse Specializing in Neonatal Care. Lisa pulled out her phone. Placing the number in her contact list, she placed the card in her wallet. She rocked back and forth. She couldn't wait to get outside and call her husband.

Chapter 13

Johnny sat at his desk. His eyes were glued to his best friend. Johnny couldn't help but be concerned about him. He knew that Mason had been through a lot. He only wished he knew how to ease Mason's pain.

Just then Johnny's phone rang. He searched around nervously. He checked his pockets and the desk drawers. He couldn't find it. Johnny knew Lisa had went to the doctor and it might be her calling. Johnny looked once more. The phone sat on the edge of the desk. Johnny laughed at himself as he answered it.

"Hello!," he said. The moment he heard Lisa's sweet voice, Johnny stepped into the hallway.

"What? Are you sure?," Mason heard Johnny asking from the other side of the door. Seconds later, Johnny came back into the office. He started pacing back and forth. He looked as if he was going to explode from the excitement.

"Is everything alright?," Mason asked concerned about Lisa and his godchild.

"Yeah man, everything's cool. Lisa is just pregnant with twins. A boy and a girl. Nothing big. So, what are we going to eat for lunch? I'm starving," Johnny said nonchalantly.

"Nothing big? She's pregnant with twins? A boy and a girl?" Mason reiterated everything Johnny said in disbelief. This was cause for celebration. He knew how long they were trying to have kids. Now Lisa was pregnant with twins.

Johnny started laughing. He could no longer contain his
excitement. Besides, it felt good to see his best friend
smiling for a change. Johnny was overjoyed. His wife was
pregnant with twins.

"You know this means Lisa and I are truly going to need
your help Mason", Johnny told him.

"I know Johnny," was the only response Mason could
give.

"Look Mason! Lisa and I were talking. We've been
worried about you and well....," he said nervously before
continuing. "We want you to come to church with us this
Sunday."

"Johnny, I love you and Lisa. I would do anything for
you two but I can't promise you that. You know I stopped
believing in God after all I've been through," Mason
responded.

"If you won't do it for me and Lisa then do it for your
godchildren," Johnny said. He was using the kids and prayed
the guilt trip would work.

"Okay I'll be there," Mason said quickly, before he
changed his mind.

"Great! Do you need the address?," Johnny asked. He
was shocked it had worked.

"No! I know where it is," Mason informed him.

"Alright I'm going to get out of here. I need to go
home and spend time with my beautiful wife. By the way
service starts at eleven," Johnny said as he grabbed his
jacket and turned off his desk light.

"Yeah! Get out of here. I'll see you Sunday," Mason
said just before the door slammed shut. He couldn't believe
he had just agreed to go to church. It had been years since
he went to one. He found himself smiling at the thought of
Johnny and Lisa having twins.

Chapter 14

The rest of the week went by without a hitch. The days literally seemed to fly by. Mason lay in bed wearing his old black and gray Army PT shorts. He had been awake for hours. It was Sunday and he didn't feel like getting out of bed. Suddenly, the alarm went off. He couldn't fight it anymore. He had to get up.

The wood floor had a chill to it. Mason darted into the bathroom. He jumped unto the shower only to realize the water was coming out ice cold. Mason could only stand it for a few minutes before he jumped out of the shower and dried off.

Mason's black suit, white shirt and tie was draped across the couch. He quickly got dressed and walked into his bedroom to find his shoes. A few minutes later Mason found the perfect pair. As he stepped into them, Mason looked out the window. He found himself worrying about his beautiful neighbor. He hadn't seen her since that day.

Mason looked down at his watch. It read exactly ten thirty. It was time to go. Mason rushed out the apartment, locked the door and hopped in the elevator. When he got outside, his 69 silver Sting Ray convertible was waiting.

Mason walked towards it. The street was desolate. No car drove down the street nor were there any children playing outside. Mason laughed. Everyone must be sleeping in late.

Mason hit the auto start button on his key ring. The car roared to life as he opened the door. Gospel was playing on the radio. Mason got in, locked the doors and fastened his seatbelt. He made sure to say his silent prayer before driving off.

A half an hour later, Mason pulled up in front if the church. He sat outside for a few. He watched as throngs of people poured inside. Once the crowd thinned out, Mason reached behind him and grabbed his Bible.

Mason got out and locked the car door behind him. It had felt like forever since he had been to church. He walked in nervously. He felt like they could smell and see the sins he had committed. Instead everyone smiled and welcomed him.

As Mason entered the sanctuary, he was ushered to his seat. Johnny and Lisa sat waiting. Mason gave both a hug and said congratulations before taking a seat beside them.

Mason looked around in awe and amazement. The sanctuary was huge. It was also packed. There was one other seat left. That seat was directly next to him.

"Lord, please don't let someone sit next to me that wants to preach ahead of the Pastor. Amen," he prayed.

His head was bowed. As he opened his eyes, he caught sight of a pair of amazing shapely legs. Whoever, they belonged to was standing right beside him. He was afraid to look and see who they belong to. After all, he didn't want to seem like a perverted old sinner in church.

"Hey Kiera, I see you made it," he heard Lisa say.

"Yes Lisa, I thought I was never going to get here. The buses are running so slow and were packed," the voice belonging to the shapely legs answered. Mason was definitely afraid to look now. He felt he had been set up. The last time that happened, the woman started stalking him.

"This is my husband Johnny. Johnny this is Kiera Williams. She's the nurse that discovered I was having twins," Lisa said as she introduced them.

"Hello Johnny," Kiera said. Her soft southern accent was intoxicating.

"This is his best friend and the kids godfather, Mason Steele," Lisa said.

Mason cut his eyes towards her and Johnny. They were both smiling. It was definitely a set up and he had walked right into it. Mason looked back at the ground and shook his head.

Grunting, Mason slowly stood up. He turned to introduce himself. He let his eyes trace the curves of her body as he raised his head. Her body was incredible. Finally, his eyes locked on her almond shaped eyes and enchanting smile. It was her but how?

Chapter 15

    Mason stared as she extended her hand. He couldn't
stop his palms from sweating. He could feel his heart
beating fast. His skin was flush. He couldn't believe it.
Here he was, a grown man acting like a nervous teenage boy.

    "Hello Mr. Steele," she said. Mason loved how it
seemed to roll off her tongue. If he was dreaming, he didn't
want to wake up.

    "Hello Kiera! Please call me Mason," he replied. She
looked absolutely breathtaking.

    "Mason," she said smiling.

    Mason reached out to shake her hand. She must have been
nervous too. Her hand was soft but sweaty. He found himself
flirtatiously rubbing her hand with his thumb. He didn't
want to let her hand go.

    Suddenly the praise team entered the sanctuary. Music
filled the room. The angelic voices of the singers broke
Kiera and Mason from their trances. Mason let go of her hand
and they both took their seats.

    Pastor Boyce came out soon after. He spoke on
forgiveness. He told his parishioners that they hold
themselves prisoner when they are unable to forgive. Mason
felt like that message was definitely for him.

Mason's mind drifted in and out during the service. He thought back to the first day, he actually saw her. He wanted to speak but some of the guys he was with started betting on who could get her in bed first. It angered him. He wanted her more than any woman he ever knew.

Mason looked briefly to his left. Kiera was listening intently to everything Pastor Boyce was saying. She took notes. He could see the light dancing in her eyes. She looked over towards him and smiled. He knew then and there, he was going to let another opportunity slip away.

As service ended, Mason excused himself and ran to the restroom. He wasn't sure if he was nervous or if he really had to go. When he finished, he washed his hands and raced back to the sanctuary.

When Mason got upstairs, Pastor Boyce was standing in the lobby. Pastor was there shaking hands. Mason hadn't seen him since Johnny and Lisa's wedding. Mason tried to blend into the crowd before Pastor Boyce saw him.

"Mason? Mason Steele?," Pastor yelled out.

"How are you?," Mason asked.

" I've been great. We haven't seen you in quite some time. I'm glad you showed up today," Pastor Boyce said.

"I am definitely thankful I showed up too. I felt like those whose words were truly for me, " Mason said to him.

"Well Brother Mason, I do hope to see you more often. God also needed me to give you a message. He wants you to know that you are about to endure a tough battle. Things will be revealed even about you. Your body, your heart and your beliefs will be tested. You will find yourself ready to give up. Don't give up. He will be in your corner and you will have a turn around," Pastor informed him.

"Well Pastor, I will definitely try my best to come more often and I thank you for those encouraging words," Mason replied as he shook the Pastor's hand. Mason had already felt like his life was under attack.

"Well brother, I'll see you next time and God bless you," the Pastor said.

"Thank you and may God continue to bless you and your family," Mason said. He then waved good bye and rushed back into the sanctuary.

When he got inside, he noticed Johnny was helping Lisa to her feet. He truly admired the love his two friends shared for one another. He hoped to find such true love one day. He raced over to give Johnny a hand.

"Where did you run off to?," Johnny asked him.

"I had to use the restroom," Mason replied.

"Mason, I am sorry I put you on the spot. She is a really nice, beautiful, intellectual, spiritual woman. I just thought she would be perfect for you," Lisa blurted out.

"What? Who are you talking about?," Mason asked.

"Kiera! You know the woman that was sitting next to you?," she answered.

"When did she leave?," he questioned as he feverishly scanned the sanctuary.

"You didn't pass her on the way back? She left a little while ago," Johnny said.

"Okay. I got to go," Mason said as he began to back peddle towards the church doors.

"Why? What's wrong?," Johnny asked, now confused.

"Do you remember the woman we helped move in a few months ago," Mason asked.

"Vaguely. Are you talking about the woman you've been scared to talk to?," Johnny inquired.

"Yes Johnny! Well it turns out that the woman Lisa invited to church today was her," Mason informed him.

Lisa stood transfixed. She was curious to know what was going on. Mason left Johnny to answer that. He ran outside as fast as possible. Many of the churchgoers were still outside walking around and talking.

Mason looked around in every direction. He doubted she was still there. He couldn't locate her anywhere in the crowd. Mason bounded down the church steps two at a time. Once at the bottom, he leaped off the last step and raced to his car. He pressed the auto start button and unlocked the car door.

The engine roared to life. Mason hopped in and checked his mirrors. Satisfied no traffic was coming, he pulled away from the curb. He didn't know where he was going but he searched he every block for her. Just then, Mason noticed the traffic light was red. He slammed down on the brakes. Mason's body lunged forward. He had forgotten to put on his seatbelt.

"What's happening to me? Mason, you are acting like a horny teenage boy. You are out of her league. She could never be interested in a man like you anyway," Mason said to himself as he stared in the rearview mirror. The light changed. Mason had talked himself out of pursuing Kiera. Suddenly, it started raining.

People scurried for cover. Cars splashed through the huge puddles, drenching people as they stood at the bus stop. Mason's eyes locked onto one in particular. Kiera had just gotten splashed by a truck as it drove by.

Mason made an illegal U-turn right in the middle of the street. He slowly eased his car into the bus stop. Grabbing the umbrella he kept for such emergencies, Mason hopped out and walked towards her.

Kiera was standing there looking at her soaked dress and hadn't seen him approach her. "Excuse me ma'am," Mason said extending his hand out to her.

"I don't mean to come off as rude or anything but, I am really not in any mood to talk," Kiera said, still not looking up to see who was talking to her.

."Well, that's quite alright. You really don't have to talk to me at all. I just wanted to offer you a ride home Miss Kiera," Mason said with a smile.

She looked up slowly. You could tell she was a bit confused as to who would be saying or even know her name. She smiled immediately when she saw Mason's face. He opened his umbrella and held it over her head. Mason swept her hair out of her face and Kiera locked her arm around his.

"So where's your car?," Kiera asked as Mason guided her around the pools of water.

56

Mason had to think about her question for a few. He thought back to the times he saw her. He realized every time he saw her, he usually was driving the Charger. When Mason looked over he saw a puzzled look on Kiera's face. He struggled not to break out in laughter.

"This is my car," Mason said as he bent down to open the door for her. "It's beautiful," Kiera said as she scanned the interior. "I'm drenched though. I don't want to ruin the leather Mr. Steele".

" Please call me Mason. We need to get you out of this rain before you get sick", Mason told her.

Kiera still was hesitant. She turned and looked at Mason nervously. Mason simply smiled, nodded and pointed to the seat. Kiera smiled back, feeling more reassured. Mason held her hand as she stepped into the car.

Once she was comfortable, Mason reached over and fastened her seat belt. He tried desperately not to stare as her rain soaked blouse clung to her her breasts. The scent of her perfume was intoxicating.

Mason could feel her breath on his face as she began breathing heavily. Mason stood up and ran over to the driver's side. Once inside Mason reached in the backseat. It only took him a few seconds to find what he was looking for. He smiled as he offered her a towel. She was shivering as she took it from his hand.

Mason reached over and turned on the heat. He took the towel from her and began to dry her hair and face with it. The heat was kicking in slowly. He rubbed his hands down her arms in an attempt to warm her up. A tingle shot through him the moment their skin touched. He found himself looking in her eyes.

As if on cue, Luther Vandross began singing "Here and Now" on the radio. Mason rested his hand on her cheek. He barely knew this woman but, he wanted to kiss her. He brushed her hair out of her face. She smiled nervously.

Just as he leaned in to kiss her, the music changed. They pulled back from each and laughed shyly. Mason turned the radio off. He looked at Kiera once more before, he placed the car in drive and headed home.

.

Chapter 16

They were so caught up in their conversation that neither of them had realized the rain had stopped. Kiera was a strong and an amazing woman. She was a survivor of domestic abuse.

When she spoke of it Mason could see the hurt in her eyes. It angered him to know that a man could ever put his hands on a woman. Mason wiped the tears from her eyes. He knew he would do his best to erase all the hurt and betrayal she felt.

He quickly changed the subject. He learned she was a neonatal nurse. She dealt with prematurity, birth defects, infections, cardiac malformations and surgical problems with newborn babies.

The passion she had for her job was unlike anything he'd ever seen. He could listen to her talk for hours. They laughed, talked and even sung a few songs. The time seemed to fly by.

Before they knew it, they were pulling into the parking shared by the tenants of their two buildings. Mason parked the car and then got out to open the door for Kiera. As she unfastened her seat belt, Mason extended his hand once again.

She looked up hesitant. He could tell she wasn't too trusting of men. He motioned for her to take his hand. She grabbed hold and he helped her out the car.

59

"I'm so sorry Mason. I'm just not used to this type of treatment," Kiera said as if reading his mind.

Hearing that troubled Mason. He was ashamed to be a man. His blood was boiling. Mason didn't know what he would do if he ever laid eyes on the man who hurt her.

He wanted to be her strength, her comforter and her protector. "It's alright Kiera. Look! I hope you know I really enjoyed talking to you and getting to know you and well....," Mason said nervously.

"Yes Mason, I've enjoyed it as well," she interrupted. Just the way she looked at him made Mason's knees weak.

"Well I was wondering if we could perhaps continue this conversation over dinner tonight at Geraldo's?," he asked.

"Geraldo's? I haven't been here long but isn't that the new restaurant that just opened? I've heard some of the nurses at the hospital talk about that place. I heard they have some amazing food but they are a little on the expensive side," she rambled on.

"Don't worry yourself about that. I would simply love the pleasure of your company over dinner and the chance to continue to get to know you better," he said as he looked into her beautiful sultry brown eyes.

"I would love that so, my answer is yes," she replied with a smile on her face.

"Great! Let's say I'll come by to pick you up around seven, if that's alright with you", Mason asked trying to remain calm, cool and collected. Deep inside, he knew he would be counting the minutes.

"That sounds perfect Mason", Kiera answered. She was barely able to contain her own excitement.

Mason continued to walk her to the door of her building. The walk felt way too short. At one point, the heel of her shoe got stuck in a crack on the sidewalk. As she was falling, she reached her hand out. Mason moved quickly and caught her in his arms. She smelled divine. He steadied her to her feet, not really wanting to let her go.

Suddenly, they heard a woman's shrill cry for help. They both looked around before realizing it came from deep within the bowels of the alleyway between their two buildings. Without thinking, Mason started running toward the alleyway. He had no idea what he was running into but he couldn't just stand there while someone needed help.

Mason looked back to see Kiera already on her cellphone, calling for help. She had a worried look on her face. Her lips seemed to be mouthing the words, "Be Careful". Seconds later, he disappeared into the alley.

Chapter 17

Mason raced around the corner unsure of what he might encounter. When he got there, Mason was disgusted at what he saw. A man lie bruised and battered on the ground. A woman was bent over a garbage dumpster with her legs spread apart. The woman's panties were ripped off and discarded on the damp ground.

A man stood on each side, pinning her arms down. Another man stood behind her with his pants around his ankles. Mason could hear the fear in her screams. The men stood there laughing. The cowards were preparing to rape her. Her eye was black and blue from the beating they had given her.

Realizing that none of the men had noticed him, Mason reached into his jacket and pulled out his baton. He quickly flung his arm out to his side. The baton extended. Mason slowly crept behind the man who had his pants down. His friends were to busy laughing and concentrating on the woman to notice him.

Mason knew he had to think fast. The man was prepared to enter her. As soon as Mason was in position, he raised the baton and rammed it into the man's groin. Almost instantly, the man clutched his manhood as he jumped up and down screaming in agony. For him to be such a big man, he screamed like a little girl.

Seeing their friend in pain, the other two released the woman and charged at Mason. One of the men swung hoping to land a blow. Mason ducked down striking him in the gut. This caused the man to double over in pain. Moving quickly, Mason swung the baton again. This time, striking the man behind the neck. The man collapsed and passed out.

The second man grabbed a lead pipe as he charged at Mason. He began swinging wildly. Mason looked for the perfect opportunity and rolled under the swing. Unfortunately, Mason dropped the baton. Seeing his chance the man began to rain blows down at Mason. Each blow crashed down into Mason's ribcage.

Mason scampered around until he found a broken glass bottle. He whirled around striking him. The glass cut into the man's face from his mouth to his ear. Blood dripped from the bottle. The man immediately dropped the pipe and grabbed at his face. Mason grabbed him by his waistband and threw him into the trash cans.

The woman ran over and hugged him. She thanked me and then ran over to the unconscious man. He was badly beaten and bloody but slowly starting to stir. The woman cried tears of joy as she attempted to help her husband up.

Mason went over and offered him a hand. Once he got up they thanked Mason again. Suddenly, a look of fear came across their faces. The suddenly started running. Mason began to turn his head to see what startled them. He was struck over the head.

He felt something warm trickling down his face. It got into his eyes, stinging and blurring his vision. Mason wiped at his eyes. It was then through squinted eyes that he saw the blood...his blood. He was starting to feel light headed. Everything was going dark. He couldn't see anymore.

Mason heard voices around him. One, two, three, four different voices. All of them belonging to men. "Four?", Mason thought to himself. Somehow he must have missed one.

Suddenly the men started pummeling him. He was being beaten within an inch of his life. They stomped on his wrists, ankles, knees and head. They also used their Steele toe boots, pipes, bricks, trash cans and even their fists to further attack Mason's ribs and the rest of his body.

63

Mason was still unable to see and rolled his body into a ball. Mason felt like he was being beaten for hours. He knew they wanted to kill him. He only hoped he passed out before they did. Just then he heard a woman's scream from the distance.

"Please stop", the woman begged of them. The voice sounded familiar to Mason. It was Kiera. e men did as she said. They stopped.

"Well, well, well! We definitely can make some time to play with you sexy lady", Mason heard one of them say.

"No! No! No! Not her," Mason screamed. He was so badly beaten that it sounded more like a whisper than a scream. Mason struggled to get back to his feet. Every time he came close, someone would knock him back down. He could hear them cackling like a bunch of hyenas.

Mason found it so hard to breathe but he needed to keep Kiera safe. Finally Mason staggered to his feet. Still blinded, he swung wildly. The men continued to laugh, as none of his swings connected. Suddenly, Mason heard the wailing sirens of police and paramedics in the distance.

Every second they were getting closer. "Kiera did it. They were coming," Mason said to himself, laughing.

"What should we do?," Mason heard one of the men ask.

The sound of their boots pounding the pavement, let Mason know they weren't going to stick around and talk to the police. Mason rolled onto his back. Droplets of rain hit his face. He couldn't see. His body ached all over. He felt a hand on him. He could hear Kiera calling his name.

"Thank God she's safe," Mason whispered before slipping into unconsciousness.

Chapter 18

When Mason woke all he could see was darkness. All he could imagine is that he lost his eye sight. He attempted to touch his face. As he raised his arms, his body felt as if he was struck by a semi. He had never felt that way before. If it wasn't for the pain, Mason would've thought he was dead.

As Mason finally touched his face, he was shocked to feel the prickliness of a full beard. How long had he been out? Where was he? Why couldn't he see? What happened? All these questions were swimming in his head. His hand inched up further until he felt the bandage covering his eyes.

Try as he might, Mason couldn't remember what happened. To be honest, he was scared. He needed to know where he was. Without thinking, Mason began clawing at his bandages.

"Well, well, well sleepyhead. I see that you're finally awake," Mason heard the soft sound of a woman's voice say joyfully. Her voice seemed soothing and a tad bit familiar. He relaxed but never took his hand off the bandages.

"Let me help you with that," she said as she rested her hands on top of his. Her hands were smooth to the touch. Soft and delicate.

"What happened?," he questioned as she gently removed his bandages.

"A couple was being attacked a few days ago. The husband lie bloody in the alley. His wife was about to be raped. You saved them," she informed him.

"Well I'm definitely happy to hear that," he said. Although he didn't remember any of it, it felt great to know he was able to help someone.

"So where am I ?, How did I get here? Why can't I remember anything? Why can't I see anything?," he rattled on question after question as he struggled to see.

She walked over, tilted his head back and dropped solution into each eye. It burned a bit. Mason closed his eyes tight, hoping to stop the pain. As he did that, she informed him of how he was blindsided by one of the assailants. Apparently, he struck Mason so hard that he slipped into a coma and suffered from short term memory loss.

The doctors also told her that the blow to his head had affected his vision. They believed it to only be temporary blindness. She volunteered to take care of him. Once the doctors learned she was a nurse, she allowed her to sign him out and take him home.

Mason sat there in awe. All this news was shocking to hear. Deep down inside Mason didn't want to believe it. There he sat though, unable to see or recollect what happened. He heard sobbing. He desperately wanted to see who had taken care of him. All he could make out was dark blurry images.

Mason could hear her walk across the room and open the blinds. The sun's rays bathed his body. He moved his hands over his chest and legs. It was then, that he realized he was naked. Embarrassed, Mason reached for something to cover himself with.

"Oh trust me Mr. Mason, you have absolutely nothing to be ashamed about," she told him. He felt a warm flush on his cheeks. He was actually blushing. He couldn't help but laugh. Mason closed his eyes tight.

When Mason opened his eyes, he could finally see. Bent over, with her back towards him, staring out of the window stood a shapely woman. She was short and thick. She also had a smooth, rich, dark chocolate complexion.

His eyes traveled up her thick thighs and over her delicious heart shaped bottom, which were encased in some red and black boy shorts. The bottom of her rear end peeked out at him. This alone, had his manhood throbbing. His gaze then fell on her tiny waist. He also noticed the sexy dimples on the small of her back. Mason grabbed the pillow and placed it in his lap as he attempted to conceal his erection.

"I'm sure you must enjoy the wonderful view you have," she said without looking back at him.

"How did she even know he was looking at her ?", he thought to himself. He pulled the covers tightly around him, hoping she wouldn't be able to see his erection.

"Huh? Umm what view?," he asked.

She whirled around. His memories of her came back instantaneously. A smile appeared on his face. It was Kiera. Seeing her made thoughts of what happened come rushing back. He remembered the thugs hitting him with anything that they could. He remembered her screams of fear and concern as he lie in a heap in the alleyway.

Mason was surprised to see her there. She barely knew him. To be honest, she was the last person he thought would take care of him. Just then, he noticed her staring at the covers gathered around his erection. Grabbing her stethoscope off the dresser, she slowly started walking towards him.

He couldn't take his eyes off of her nor the hypnotic sway of her hips. She stopped, now standing directly between his legs. Kiera smiled down at him. She then, placed the chest piece of the stethoscope over his heart and grabbed his wrist to check his pulse.

Try as he might to look away, Mason's attention was drawn to the opening in her blouse. She had on a red and black lace bra. A heart shaped pendant lie in the center of it. His heart rate quickened.

His gaze remained transfixed on her breasts. The scent of her perfume was intoxicating. He was certain she could feel his manhood throbbing against her leg. He shyly looked up only to have her catch him staring.

"It's great to know that you can see again. Judging by your umm vitals, I gather you like what you see Mr. Mason," Kiera said jokingly. She was staring into his eyes. She had a sexy, playful smile on her face.

"Hold on now!," he exclaimed. He was still amazed at the raspy, garbled sound of his voice. "Just when exactly did I go from Mason to Mr. Mason?," he asked.

"Oh! That's easy to answer. The moment you became my patient Mr. Mason. I take my work very seriously and I don't mix business with pleasure, " she replied. Teasing him she walked back to the window and looked out.

"Is that how you address all of your patients Miss Kiera?," Mason asked sarcastically.

"If you really must know sir, most of my patients are infants but yes I address all my patients in the same manner," she replied. "However Mr. Mason, I must admit you are definitely the first patient I had, that I enjoyed giving a sponge bath," Kiera added as she looked seductively over her left shoulder.

"So that's where my clothes went," Mason though to himself. Too bad he was unconscious at the time. He was sure he would have enjoyed being her patient. Mason couldn't help blushing at the thought of her hands bathing him.

"Why Mr. Mason, am I going to have to sit you in a tub of ice water?," she questioned.

"Why Nurse Kiera? Is there something wrong?," Mason asked trying to look nervous and concerned. He knew she was taunting him and decided to play along.

"Well Mr. Mason, your face seems to have taken on a bit of color. Perhaps, you're coming down with a fever. Let me check," she said before biting her lower lip. Mason only wished he could bite it for her.

For the first time in his life, Mason was nervous around a woman. Oh he definitely believed he had a fever. A fever of uncontrollable passion. A fiery fever for the woman in front of him.

Kiera began to look around. Unable to find what she needed, she sensuously walked towards him. He didn't believe she truly understood what she was doing to him. Maybe she did. She stood mere inches in front of him. Her hands were on her hips. She leaned over. Her cleavage teased him once more.

Kiera placed her hand gently on his forehead, cheeks, neck and chest. He enjoyed the way she touched him. He placed his hands on his lap. Secretly, Mason wished her hand traveled even lower.

She must have been psychic or maybe she actually knew what she was doing to him. Suddenly, she moved her hand down to his abs. Her hand gently brushed the head of his shaft. She looked into his eyes and smiled as Mason let out a low passionate moan.

"Well everything definitely feels fine to me," she said, again biting her lip.

"I want to thank you Miss Kiera for taking care of me," Mason said.

"It was truly a pleasure. Now that you are you're feeling better, I can head home and get ready for my date," she said excitedly as she looked him up and down.

"Oh! You have a date?," Mason asked disappointedly. Deep down he wondered if his jealously showed.

"Yeah! I've been waiting on him for quite some time. It seems he finally noticed me," she responded.

"Raise your arms so I can wrap those ribs Mr. Mason. As a matter of fact, how about you stand up so I can secure it better," she ordered.

Mason looked down nervously. He then grabbed the bed sheet and attempted to tie it around his waist. He then tugged at it. When he was certain it was secure, Mason stood up.

"You will have to move that out of the way Mr. Mason and please hurry" she instructed him.

Mason loosened his the sheet and watched it fall to the floor. Kiera looked down and smiled. He stood there, feeling helpless and embarrassed. He expected her to make some sort of lewd comment. Instead, she wrapped the bandage around his ribs. Satisfied it was secure, she walked out the room in search of her keys.

"Is it alright if I pick up the rest of my things?," she asked, screaming it from somewhere in the apartment.

Mason attempted to yell back when suddenly she popped her head back in the room. She tilted her head to the side. He thought it was so cute, that he lost his train of thought. They stood there for a few minutes just staring at one another.

"Well ???," she started to ask with a smile on her face.

"Oh sure!," Mason stammered and continued. "You can come back for them anytime."

Happy with his answer, Kiera turned on the balls of her feet and disappeared into the living room. Mason scooped up the sheet and fastened it around her waist.

By the time, he had gotten to the living room, Kiera had on her workout pants and sneakers. She smiled and looked at him. She then walked over to the apartment door.

"I hope to see you later," she said before closing the door behind her.

Chapter 19

Mason stood in the middle of the living room just staring at the door. He so desperately wanted it all to be a joke. He wanted the door to swing open and hear her say she was just kidding. It didn't. He waited a few minutes before he truly believed she was gone.

So many thoughts and emotions were running through his mind. He needed to sit down. Kiera must have slept there on the couch because beside him was some sheets, a blanket, and three pillows. She also left her uniforms, work shoes and a gym bag with sexy panties and bras.

Confused, Mason sat there looking at the things she left behind. He had wanted her every since he laid eyes on her. He finally had gotten up the courage, she said yes and then he had to rush off and play hero. She was here for who knows how many days just taking care of him. Now she was out there with some other man.

Anger was starting to build up inside of him. It wasn't fair. He waited so long for her. He wanted to be mad at her. How could she go out with someone else? How could she cheat on him? He was even mad at himself. How could he just let her walk out that door and into the arms of another man. He was so mad that he wanted to scoop her clothes up and toss them into the hallway.

Suddenly, Mason let out a loud raucous laugh. He was shocked at how he was acting. Here he was was actually getting jealous and angry. He needed to pull himself together. He barely even knew this woman and she had him talking to himself.

Just then, his stomach started growling. He was absolutely starving. Mason eased himself off the couch and made a beeline for the kitchen. His ribs ached with each step. On the counter was a brand new prescription bottle of Percocet. Seeing it took him back to his military days. "Hmm Ranger candy," Mason thought to himself. He remembered how they would give them that for everything.

He desperately needed one right now. His stomach growled even louder. Maybe God was reminding him that he shouldn't take medicine on an empty stomach. Mason literally felt like his stomach was touching his back. He needed food and he needed it now.

He opened the pantry only to discover cans of soup and vegetables. He wanted something quick so, looking in the freezer was out of the question. He opened the refrigerator. It seemed barren. Mason was prepared to give up hope but as he squatted down his eyes caught sight of something.

He saw a Ziploc bag with some cold cuts in it, a piece of cheese and a small bottle of his favorite vanilla Chai tea. The label on the outside read Teriyaki roasted chicken. He pulled everything out. There was just two pieces of meat left. Just enough for him to make one sandwich.

Although, Mason didn't have any mayonnaise or mustard, he managed to devour the sandwich in two bites. He was hurting but still hungry. He knew he needed to do some grocery shopping. He made a quick shopping list and headed to take a shower.

As he stepped into the living room Mason's attention was drawn to Kiera's belongings. Thinking of her out with another man was depressing. He wanted it to be him. He slowly placed her stuff in the closet, hoping putting it away would take his mind off her.

Once everything was put away Mason walked into the bathroom. He sat on the edge of the tub and turned on the faucet. The water came out steaming hot. Way too hot for him. Mason turned on the cold water a bit to cool it down.

He was finally satisfied with the temperature. He unwrapped the sheet from around him. It was then that he remembered he was bandaged. He could only shake his head as he realized he couldn't take a shower. He turned the shower off and began washing up in the sink instead.

With his ribs aching it took Mason longer than he expected. Once finished, he walked through the apartment naked. He had just gotten his underwear and socks on when he heard sounds coming from the living room. It sounded like talking.

Mason grabbed the black aluminum bat in the corner of the room. He then slowly crept towards the living room. From where he was, he noticed that the television was on. He couldn't help but wonder if he had locked the door. He tightened his grip on the bat, raised it high in the air and proceeded further into the living room.

The living room was empty. Did he leave the T.V. on? Was it on before and he hadn't noticed? Mason grabbed the remote off the arm of the couch. He then turned the T.V. off. He then walked over to the door and made sure it was locked.

He had an uneasy feeling in the pit of his stomach. He searched behind the bar, in the bathroom, spare bedroom and closets. He didn't find anyone. Maybe he had cut it on. Maybe he was imagining things. He started to laugh at himself when suddenly, he heard a noise coming from the kitchen.

As he approached the kitchen he heard footsteps. They were coming closer. Mason propped himself against the wall, raising the bat he prepared to swing. A shrill scream filled the air. He stopped mid swing. Kiera stood there terrified. Mason dropped and pulled her into his arms.

"What are you doing here? Did your date cancel?," he asked secretly hoping her date did.

"Why aren't you dressed? Why did you almost take my head off?," she questioned him back. He could feel her shaking in his arms.

"I apologize for scaring you. I thought someone was breaking in. Now please tell me, what I should be getting dressed for?," Mason asked.

"Our date", she answered as she pushed out of his arms.

"Our date?," Mason repeated as he cocked his head to the side,a bit confused.

"Yes you idiot! Who did you think I was waiting to go out with?," Kiera yelled as she placed her hands on her hips and moved her head from side to side.

Mason stepped back and stared at her. For the first time he noticed what she was wearing. Kiera stood there wearing a red top with a plunging neck line. It tied around her waist. She also had on a black skirt that flared out and some incredibly beautiful black suede booties that showcased her legs.

Thoughts of her in just those booties and a smile filled his head. Mason smiled. He was the man she wanted to go out with. Just then, Mason remembered that he was still standing in his underwear. Without saying a word, he ran out the room to find something to wear.

"Now what?," Kiera yelled. "Should I just leave?"

"No! No! No! Just give me a few seconds to put something on and we'll go," he replied, shouting from the bedroom.

Mason found his grey shirt, black, grey and white tie, black dress pants and leather shoes. Just that movement drained him. He hurt but he wasn't going to miss this chance. He hadn't felt this excited about anyone in a long time.

"Kiera!," he called out.

"Yes Mason, are you alright?", she asked. He could here her footsteps coming down the hall.

"Could I ask for your help putting on my shirt?", he asked just as she stepped into the room.

Kiera smiled and grabbed his wife beater T-shirt off the bed. She slid it over his head, placing her hands on his side as he raised his arms to put it on. She then reached down to pick up his grey shirt. Mason slid his arms into the shirt. Once it was on Kiera began buttoning it. They never took their eyes off of each other.

Completely satisfied with how he looked, Mason grabbed his wallet, keys and phone from the nightstand. He also grabbed a jacket in case it got cold. They then headed for the door. Mason pulled out his keys to lock the door but to his surprise, Kiera was already locking it.

It didn't bother him that she had keys. Mason leaned against the wall watching, waiting and smiling. He watched as she checked to make sure the door was locked and then placed the keys in her purse. She looked so comfortable with them that Mason started to wonder where she had gotten the keys from and how long she had them. As if she read his thoughts Kiera grabbed hold of his hand and started talking.

"When you got hurt, I immediately called Lisa. Her and Johnny came rushing over. They were going to take turns nursing you back to health but, with her pregnancy I argued against that and besides, I am better trained. Once I assured them that I would stay, Johnny had a copy of the keys made," Kiera informed him.

Mason simply shook his head and nodded. He was speechless. He hardly knew this beautiful woman in front of him yet she took time to take care of him. He would definitely have to make sure to thank Johnny if all of this works out. Hr must of been daydreaming for quite a while because when he finally looked at her, Kiera was standing there staring at him.

"Mason are you alright? If you're hurting I understand. We can always reschedule that way you can stay home and relax," she said with heartfelt concern.

"Oh I am so sorry Kiera. I had something on my mind," he replied.

   "What is it Mason? Is it the key?," she asked as she opened her purse and took out the key. "You can have them back if you want. I mean, now that you're better I won't really need them, will I ?"

   Mason didn't know which one of them was more confused. He didn't want the key back. He wanted to get to know her. Most of all, he wanted her. He just couldn't say it. It was too soon.

   "If you don't mind can you hold onto the key a little longer. See I'm still sore and it would me a lot to me if you checked on me," Mason told her.

   The smile that appeared on her face was priceless. Mason pressed the button for the elevator as she put the key away. He couldn't take his eyes off of the undeniable vision of beauty that stood before him. She was amazing.

   Just then the elevator arrived. Mason held the door so that she could get in first. The elevator was packed. More people continued to get on as the elevator made its descent to the lobby. Mason hated crowds but as long as Kiera's body was pressed against his, he wouldn't dare complain. She placed her hand on his chest. The moment he looked into those honey brown almond shaped eyes nothing and no one else mattered.

   The elevator finally stopped on the first floor. Mason pulled Kiera closer. The others passengers stampeded towards the open doors. He looked at her. Their eyes locked. He longed to kiss her but knew they had to go.

   Mason took Kiera by the hand. The crowd waiting to get on was thick. Despite them repeatedly saying "Excuse us," the crowd relentlessly bumped them around as if they were in a pinball machine. Maintenance was on the way to fix the other two elevators.

Once in the lobby, Mason straightened out his clothes and searched for Dexter. Dex sat nervously behind the front desk. He seemed to be mumbling to himself. Something was different.

"Hey Dex!," Mason shouted.

Dexter raised his head midway and looked at Mason. He gave Mason a quick wave and lowered his head once more. He was sweating profusely. Something was definitely wrong.

Mason headed over to the front desk. Just then the phone rang. Dexter picked it up and started whispering. Mason didn't really want to interrupt because the call seemed personal but he needed to know his friend wasn't in any trouble.

"Hey Dex!, Are you alright?," "How is your daughter doing?", Mason whispered.

"Yeah, yeah everything is fine. Baby girl is away visiting family. You know I just really miss her though. I appreciate you stopping by to check on me Mr. Steele", Dexter whispered as he placed his hand over the phone.

" Okay if you are sure but if you need me for anything please don't hesitate to call me or stop up at my apartment," Mason said before turning and walking back to Kiera.

Kiera stood patiently waiting by the wall. Men would walk by vying for her attention. Her eyes were focused on Mason. He loved it.

Just as Mason walked up another man stopped to talk to her. The man didn't even notice Mason standing behind him. Mason watched Kiera's reaction as the man rambled on. Kiera simply stood there smiling.

"So do you have a boyfriend?," the man asked.

"Oh not yet," she answered still smiling.

"Great so there's no need to look any further love," he said as he flashed her a smile. His gold tooth shining in the light.

"Trust me when I say, I have no plans on ever looking further," she stated as she looked past him and raised an eyebrow.

Mason was so amused by the conversation. He smiled back at Kiera. Mason couldn't blame the man for trying. She was absolutely beautiful. So let's stop playing games and maybe we can get out of here," he said as he got straight to the point.

"Hey Dee," Mason called from behind him.

Dee whirled around a bit startled at first. "Hey Mason, what's going on? I was just standing here talking to this beautiful, sexy woman," he said, pointing to Kiera.

"She definitely is beautiful Dee but she's with me," Mason said as he walked past him and grabbed her hand.

"I'm so sorry Mason. She was standing here by herself looking so sexy. Can you blame me for trying?," he said apologetically.

"Definitely not Dee. I would've probably had done the same thing," Mason told him. "I don't want to seem rude Dee but we're running a little late for our dinner date."

"I understand Mason. I got you. Go take that sexy lady out of here before I steal her away," Dee said jokingly.

Taking her by the waist, Mason began to do just that. Once at the door, he stopped to hold it and wait for her to walk out. When he looked back, Mason noticed Dee was still watching and drooling over her. Dexter however, had managed to disappear somewhere. Mason hoped his friend would be alright. Closing the door behind him, Mason took Kiera's hand in his as they walked into the crisp night air.

Chapter 20

Dexter hid inside the office. He hid behind the door and peeked through the window that looked out into the lobby. He knew not to make any sudden movement or sound that might draw Mason's attention. He couldn't bring himself to even look at his old friend.

When Dexter's wife had passed due to complications with her pregnancy, Dexter had hit rock bottom. At that time, he didn't even have enough money to pay for her funeral. He couldn't even find a job then. He did whatever he had to, to make ends meet.

Dexter owed Mason everything. He didn't know how, but Mason paid for his wife's funeral. It might seem cliche to say but, getting caught was the best thing to happen to him. The night he broke into the pharmacy, a silent alarm was triggered. The police showed up in a matter of minutes.

His daughter was two months old at the time. He was on his third strike and facing life without parole. He couldn't afford a lawyer. The state had taken his daughter and placed her in foster care.

Jail was rough. Dexter had witnessed and heard stories of other prisoners fighting, killing and raping one another. His cellmate had even hung himself one night. Dexter was paranoid. He believed with his injuries, he might be the next one they came after.

Dexter didn't feel like he could trust anyone while he was in jail. He showered with his clothes on. He made sure he always used the bathroom stall instead of the urinals. He would walk down the halls sideways with his back against the wall. During chow he would sit alone at the one table that faced the entire cafeteria. He even made sure he hid shanks on his body. He knew no matter what, he wasn't going to go down without a fight.

One day, as Dexter sat alone in his cell, a guard showed up. The guard told him he had a visitor. Dexter hadn't had a visitor since he got there. He was curious to know who it was.

"Excuse me guard, may I ask who came to see me?," Dexter asked nervously.

"A Mr. Charles Stanwick," the guard replied.

"Who is that?, I don't know anyone by that name," Dexter said somewhat frightened.

"The gentleman says he's your lawyer," the guard quickly said in response.

"My lawyer? I never contacted a lawyer," Dexter said to him.
"Well we checked his credentials and he is a lawyer. In fact, he's one of the best. He usually takes on million dollar clients. We believed he was appointed by the state or doing some pro bono work until he said something rather strange," the guard informed him.

"Strange? How strange?," Dexter asked now shaken.

"He said to tell you he was his brother's keeper," the guard responded.

Dexter quickly began to relax. He wasn't sure at that time exactly who the lawyer was but, he did know he was a friend. Dexter hopped off his bunk and put on his sneakers. He then, placed his arms through the slot on his cell's door. The guard placed the handcuffs on his wrists. Dexter immediately moved back so that the guard could open the door.

The cell door opened slowly. Dexter was still somewhat hesitant to come out. He felt a lot safer in his cell. Knowing he had to go meet the lawyer, he stepped out. The guard instructed Dexter to walk in front of him.

Dexter did exactly ad he was told. Shortly after, they arrived at the visitor's area. Once there, the guard took off the handcuffs and ushered Dexter inside. Dexter stood and looked around nervously. He didn't exactly know who he was looking for. Suddenly, he saw an old familiar face.

Dexter slowly walked towards him. The man's head was down. Without looking up, the man called Dexter's name. Dexter responded. The man looked up smiling. Dexter immediately recognized him.

"Hey Harvard! You've come a long way since the war. We always knew you would make it. How did you know I was here though?," Dexter asked.

Stanwick told him everything , from the time he received the call. Mason had found a way to keep tabs on everyone. He then informed Dexter that he was working on getting him released. He also reassured him that he would get his daughter back.

A week later, Dexter was being released. He hadn't made many friends while there and couldn't wait to get out of there. Just as he was preparing to leave Officer Johnson popped in. Johnson was the one person who always seemed to watch over him and they had become good friends.

"Hey Turner, I see you're out of here," Officer Johnson said.

"Yeah finally thank God. My next step is to get my daughter back," Dexter replied.

"Well then, just make sure you don't come back," Johnson said sternly.

"Oh trust me I won't," Dexter responded quickly. "Look I know it was simply your job but, thank you for keeping me alive in here. Thank you also for listening."

"No problem!," he said as he escorted Dexter outside to an awaiting vehicle. " After all, I am my brother's keeper."

Dexter was in shock. Officer Johnson simply smiled though and walked away. The prison gates shut behind him. The sound was a chilling reminder of where Dexter had spent the last few years of his life.

The car door opened. In the back was Mason and a beautiful little girl. His little girl. It felt like forever since he had laid eyes on his daughter. She looked just like her mother. Seeing her brought tears to his eyes. She had grown so much. He missed a lot of years of her life.

The little girl looked at Dexter and then at Mason. Mason nodded. The little girl grabbed a tissue and headed toward Dexter. As he wiped the tears away, she placed her hand on his cheek.

"Thank you Selena," Dexter said.

"You're welcome but why are you crying?," Selena asked.

"I'm crying because you look so beauty. I've missed you. You look so much like your mother. Daddy loves you and I promise I will never leave you again," he told her as he kissed the palm of her hand.

"Please don't cry daddy," she said now sobbing herself.

Dexter wanted to grab hold of her and never let her go. He was shocked that she knew who he was. He would never forget that day. Mason gave him his life back. That happened six years ago.

Selena was now eighteen and a week from graduating. He was so proud of her. She was going to be her class Valedictorian and headed to medical school to be a pediatrician.

Just the other day, he took her shopping for a prom dress. Today, he gets a call no father ever wants to get. His daughter has been kidnapped. He knows if he doesn't do what the caller said, he will never see his beloved daughter again.

Dexter stood outside Mason's apartment now conflicted. He desperately wished he had told Mason. He was far too afraid of the police to ever call them. The man on the phone threatened to kill his daughter if he talked to anyone. Dexter had nowhere to turn. If he didn't do what he was told, she was dead. Selena was all he had. He couldn't lose her too.

Dexter pulled the keys off his belt loop. He searched through all the apartment keys until he found the right one and unlocked the door. He slowly opened the door and slipped inside before anyone spotted him. He then, dug into his pockets and retrieved a camera and flashlight.

As Dexter moved the light around the room, he had to laugh. He remembered how even when they served in the military together Mason had to have order. Some things apparently never change.

Dexter slipped his gloves on and began his search. He made sure he was real careful. Mason had a knack for knowing when something was touched. Since he didn't know what he was looking for, Dexter took pictures of anything and everything that might seem important.

Once Dexter finished he made sure he back tracked his steps. He wanted to be certain that he didn't miss anything. He also needed to make sure nothing was out of place. He then opened the door and eased into the hallway.

Dexter pulled the door shut behind him and ran to the elevator. He looked around nervously as he waited for the elevator to arrive. When it did, Dexter jumped in. He didn't even wait for the doors to completely open. Once inside, he pressed his body against the wall as he feverishly pressed the button to close the elevator doors.

He had survived many missions yet this one scared him the most. He knew what Mason was capable of. He also knew he had no choice. Until, he could hold his daughter in his arms again nothing else mattered.

Dexter was so jittery that he found himself looking around even after the doors closed. The elevator began its descent. He was rattled every time the doors opened. He found himself staring at everyone that got on.

He wondered if they had something to do with the abduction of his daughter. The way they looked back at him made him feel like they knew what he had done. He hung his head in shame.

Just then, the elevator doors sprung open. When Dexter looked up, he could see the lobby. Suddenly, Dexter's phone rang startling him. He checked to see who it was. It was an unknown number.

"H-h-h-hello!," Dexter answered nervously.

 "Good evening Mr. Turner. Do you have something for me or do we have to see your little girl on the news tonight?," the voice on the other end of the phone asked.

Dexter reached in his pocket and pulled out the camera. He hated betraying his friend. He really didn't want to make the trade but his back was against the wall. He knew if he didn't make the trade Selena was going to die.

"Yeah I have it. Please don't do anything to my daughter," Dexter begged.

"As long as you do exactly as I tell you then I won't. Now this is what I want you to do...the man said preparing to tell him but was interrupted.

"How do even know you have her? How do I know she's alive and that you won't kill her?," Dexter questioned.

The man walked towards Selena. She was beautiful. He knew all about Dexter and his daughter. He didn't want to have to kill her.

"This sure is a sexy yellow crop top, tight light blue low rider jeans and thigh high boots you have on," the man told her. He wanted to make sure it was loud enough for Dexter to hear.

The man began to slowly run his fingers through her hair. Selena squirmed in an attempt to get away from his touch. He didn't like to be rejected. He yanked her hair so hard that he nearly pulled some out. He enjoyed the sound of her muffled cries for help.

The man then took out his knife. He cut the gag off Selena's mouth. She sat there whimpering. She wanted to run but knew she would never make it. Tears streamed down her face. Selena was scared that she would never see her father again.

He took the tip of the knife and traced it over her breasts and down to her stomach. He spun the tip in her belly button. She winced. The whole time his eyes never left hers. Her fear fueled his fire.

"I'll tell you this...If your dear, sweet daddy doesn't bring me what I asked for soon, me and you will have some fun of our own," the man said to Selena. He then tapped the tip of his knife against her dolphin belly ring.

Selena let out a deafening scream. Dexter knew it was his daughter. She was terrified. He felt his anger boiling inside. He couldn't bare the thought of a man hurting any woman especially his baby girl...his daughter.

"Okay, Okay, Stop! Please stop it!," Dexter pleaded into the phone. "I have exactly what you asked for. Just tell me where you would like me to meet you".

Hearing that the man placed the phone back to his ear. "Meet me in the alley on the side of the building in two minutes. Remember you are still being watched so don't try anything. If you aren't there by then...," the man said pausing. "You will never see your daughter again. Oh and by the way, you now have a minute left. Tick tock Mr. Turner tick tock."

Suddenly, the man's maniacal laugh rang through Dexter's ears. Dexter needed to get his daughter back quickly. Once he had her back and safely hidden, he would stop at nothing to hunt the man down. His adrenaline took over. Dexter took off running. His injured, battered body ached with each step.

When Dexter reached the alley, he saw a white van waiting. There were no license plates on it. The windows appeared to have a dark limousine type tint. The only sound he could hear was the rumble of the van's engine.

Dexter stopped briefly. He had no idea what he was walking into. He found himself praying. He then looked down at his watch. He had mere seconds left.

He looked around for anything he could use as a weapon. Unfortunately, he didn't anything. Admittedly frightened, he slowly walked towards the van. As soon as he was close enough Dexter realized the front seat was empty.

Without warning, the back door swung open. Dexter jumped back startled. From inside, he heard that familiar evil laugh. He also could hear his daughter's muffled cries for help.

Two figures exited the vehicle. Dexter focused his attention on his daughter first. Her clothes were in a disarray. He could tell she had been crying uncontrollably. The man's arm was around her neck.

"Are you alright?," Dexter mouthed to her.

Selena nodded as she fought back the tears. Dexter then focused his attention on his daughter's kidnapper. The man appeared fit. Dexter was unsure of his height. He may have been five foot ten inches tall. He had dirty blonde hair and icy blue eyes with a sinister stare. The man also had a small swastika tattoo on the back of his hand.

Dexter figured he had at least a hundred pounds on him. Dexter wanted to rush him. He knew he could take him but couldn't risk his daughter being hurt.

"Good job Mr. Turner. I see you arrived on time. Now do you have what I asked for or am I going to have to hurt daddy's little girl?," the man asked as he looked at Dexter and smiled.

"No! Please don't hurt my daughter. I have what you asked for right here," Dexter said as he dug in his pocket for the camera.

Once he retrieved it from his pocket, Dexter slowly walked towards them. He extended his arm outward. He hoped to get close enough to grab his daughter. He feared that once the man had what he needed, he would kill Dexter's daughter.

"Whoa, whoa, whoa Mr. Turner. If I was you I wouldn't move any further. Place everything on the ground and step away," the man instructed him. Dexter did just as instructed. The man surveyed everything. When he was satisfied, he released Selena. With tears in her eyes, she rushed to her father. They held each other tight.

Dexter released his hold long enough to inspect his daughter. Certain she had no injuries. Dexter took her by the hand. "Let's get away from here as quick as possible," Dexter told her.

Selena nodded in agreement. Dexter was still unsure about what was going on. He did know something crazy was about to go down though. Knowing that, he had to get his daughter somewhere safe.

Dexter and Selena turned around. He would do whatever it took to keep her safe. They started running. Just before they were completely out of the alley, Dexter stopped to look back. He didn't want to forget the stranger's face.

Dexter knew that if he ever laid eyes on that man again he would try to kill him. Satisfied he had the guy's description, Dexter ran to catch up with his daughter. Neither of them stopped running until they reached his car. Dexter looked around.

He wanted to be certain that he wasn't being followed. Realizing he wasn't, Dexter got into the car and started the engine. He drove as fast as he could. to get out of there.

Meanwhile, in the alley the stranger looked around. He then went and sat back in the van. Patiently he watched and waited. He needed to be certain he wasn't being set up. He didn't like the feeling that crept over him.

He sat questioning his own behavior. Would he have killed the girl? What he was after wasn't just worth billions but would crush Mason Steele. He smiled. He was thankful that he wasn't forced to find out.

After waiting and contemplating five more minutes, he got out of the van. He walked slowly towards the camera. He looked around once more before picking it up. He began walking back towards the van. Out of the corner of his eye he saw something shining a few inches away.

He walked over to it and kneeled down slowly. He scanned the area to see if it was safe. Without looking down he felt around on the ground for a few seconds. Finally, he felt a large ring with keys on it. The man scooped them up and shoved it into his pocket. He smiled hoping they might prove useful.

He then rushed back toward the van. Once safely inside, he ripped off his disguise as he laughed. He stepped down on the accelerator and raced out of the alley. He desperately wanted to know what was on the camera.

Chapter 21

Mason couldn't believe it was finally happening. For months, he had wanted this woman and now she sat just inches away. Her perfume was intoxicating. They were actually going on a date.

They sat at a red light. Mason found himself staring at her legs. Thick sexy legs were always his weakness. Nervously, he allowed his eyes to trace her curves. When they made their way upwards, they were greeted by her enchanting smile.

Suddenly, he heard the blaring sounds of car horns. The light was green. Mason realized he was on Rawlins Avenue. He drove up two more blocks and made a left. They had arrived.

Kiera looked up in awe. Hearing about Geraldo's paled in comparison to actually seeing it. It was a huge beautiful white building with bay windows. Two large potted ferns were on each side of the door. A red carpet ran from the door's entrance to the curb.

Kiera was so in awe of the place that she didn't notice Mason standing with her door open. He extended his hand. A young light skinned gentleman stood beside him. She took Mason's hand and stepped out of the car. Was she dreaming? Kiera felt like royalty. Mason closed the door behind her. The young man dashed around the car and settled behind the wheel.

Kiera looked at the line of people waiting to get in. Just then she remembered her coworkers mentioning that if you didn't have reservations for this place, a person could find themselves waiting for hours. She didn't make any. She was afraid that they wouldn't get in and started pouting.

Mason caught sight of it. He fought back the urge to suck on her lips. Instead, he gently took her in his arms. He wanted to know she was alright.

"What's the matter? That lip is too tempting to poke out. If you keep doing that I will have to bite it," he whispered in her ear.

Kiera looked up at him and smirked. She liked being in his arms. She wanted to stay there forever. More than anything she wanted his mouth on hers.

"Moving a little fast there Mr. Steele. Besides, did you expect that corny line to work anyway?," she replied.

"Okay, okay", Mason said slowly backing away. He raised his hands high as he smiled. "You got me! It wasn't intended to be a line. It did make you smile though."

"That it did Mr. Steele," she said laughing. "I was just looking at the line to get in and well....."

"What is it baby?," he questioned. The word slipped out of his mouth before he could stop it.

Kiera pretended not to hear it but inside, she was doing cartwheels. He called her baby. She wanted to be his baby. She wanted to be his forever.

Taking a deep breath Kiera continued speaking, " What I was going to say is...maybe we should go somewhere else. The line is so long. We would have to wait for hour just to get in."

"Don't worry your beautiful little self," Mason replied.

"We don't have any reservations and...," she said before being interrupted.

"Kiera my love, trust me. We won't need a reservation," Mason said confidently. He then stuck his arm out.

"Did he really call me his love?," Kiera asked herself. How she only wished. Mason could have any woman he wanted but he was there with her. She must be dreaming.

"Uh hmm!", she heard. Kiera was shaken from her trance. She looked around. Mason was standing there with his arm extended. She wasn't dreaming. This was real. She wrapped her arm around his as they headed towards the door.

As they approached the doors swung open. A well manicured gentleman stood in the doorway.

"Welcome to Geraldo's. Do you have a reservation sir?," the man asked. His eyes were staring a hole through Mason.

"No sir, but I'm sure we can work something out," Mason replied as he reached into his pocket.

"Well we have quite a long line sir", the man informed him, while he looked at Kiera from the corner of his eye.

"Will this help?," Mason asked as he took his hand out of his pocket.

Kiera thought, Mason was going to pay to get in. Instead, he offered the man a coin. The man looked at it and smiled. Kiera was confused. From what she could see the coin had no value however, the man took it and shoved it in his pocket.

"Great to see you again Lieutenant Steele," the man said.

"Lieutenant Steele?," Kiera whispered under her breath.

Why did that name seem familiar? Kiera thought real hard. She had heard it before. She remembered seeing a coin like his somewhere else It had been years though. She wondered if he was the same person she was thinking of.

"Kiera Williams, this is Richard Eason", Mason said introducing them.

"Oh so you two know each other?," she asked.

Lieutenant Steele...I mean Mason pretty much saved me. I would follow him to the ends of this Earth, " he responded.

Kiera smiled. She was delighted to know she finally had a selfless, caring man who was respected by others instead of feared. Suddenly, she laughed. This was only their first date and here she was claiming him.

"I was only doing what's right. People have a way of using one another and then they discard them like yesterday's trash. When that happens society turns its nose up at one another. I vowed I would never do that to another human being," Mason told her.

Mason then shook his friend's hand. Afterwards he placed his arm around Kiera's waist. A tingle went up her spine. He seemed to be handsome, in great shape, caring, respectful and respected. He was also a modest, smart, take charge type of man. What turned her on most of all was that Mason was a gentleman. He seemed too good to be true.

Mason opened the next set of doors. Kiera was awed by the ambiance. The entire restaurant was decorated in red, silver and white. Beautiful red tapestry hung in every corner. A gentleman playing the piano was in the center of the room under a glass ceiling.

Women watched Mason as he maneuvered Kiera around the room. He exuded confidence in every stride of his step. Waitresses tried to get his attention. "Why me?," Kiera thought. "Mason could have any woman he desires so why me? As she saw all the attention Mason was getting she tried not to get jealous.

She averted her attention to the décor. Mason held her closer. To him, he was already with the sexiest woman in the room. Kiera was the one he wanted. Kiera was completely

swept away. Mason had maneuvered her to the back of the elegant restaurant. They were now standing near the elevator. She watched as the doors opened. Mason quickly ushered her inside before they closed.

"Where are we going?," she asked.

"You'll see in a minute," was his only response.

Just then, the doors opened. What Kiera saw was amazing. Just like upstairs the walls were white but with gold trim. There was a huge fish tank in the walls. The fish almost seemed to glow. A chandelier hung in the center of the room. When she looked down she noticed the rose petal trail that led to a solitary table. The table was covered by a white tablecloth with gold trimming. Gold napkins in the shape of swans sat on the table. Two crystal wine glasses also sat on the table.

A short, stout gentleman stood waiting to greet them. "Mason my dear old friend, how are you?," the man asked.

' "Feeling like I got hit by a truck," Mason replied.

He released her long enough to give the man a hug. "Geraldo this is Ms. Kiera Williams. Kiera this is my good friend Geraldo," Mason said introducing them.

He then took Kiera's hand in his. Geraldo looked at her with a stone hard stare. Nervously, she gulped. He slowly walked over to her. She tightened her grip on Mason's hand.

In one quick motion, Geraldo scooped her off the ground. He gave a her a huge hug and started to laugh. Mason laughed shortly after. Feeling a bit foolish and unsure of what to do, Kiera found herself laughing as well.

"It is truly an honor to meet such a beautiful woman," Geraldo said, placing her gently back on the ground.

"Why thank you for the compliment Mr. Geraldo," Kiera responded as she giggled nervously.

A strange look suddenly appeared on Geraldo's face. He looked at Mason. Then he looked at Kiera. Then once again back at Mason. As if Mason knew what he was thinking Mason blurted out, "She's from Tennessee."

"Beautiful and respectful. I like her already. I may have to go there and find me a good woman. Do me a favor though Kiera, call me Geraldo or Gerald," he said.

"Okay," she said with a smile "Dinner's almost ready. Please have a seat and I'll bring it right out," Geraldo said before turning to walk to the kitchen.

Kiera turned to take a seat only to find Mason pulling the chair out for her. A beautiful vase of flowers sat in the center. The waiter brought over a bowl of Caesar salad. Mason was very attentive. He served her a bowl of salad and asked if she would like some wine. It had seemed like so long since a man was concerned with her happiness. Part of her wondered if it was all a show to get her in his bed.

Kiera hadn't drank alcohol in quite a long time. She felt perhaps a glass would help her unwind. It had a wonderfully sweet taste. She decided she would have another.

They began talking. It was as if they were old friends catching up with one another. Suddenly, music filled the room. Kiera started dancing in her seat. It was Boyz II Men's "I'll Make Love To You ." Mason couldn't help but watch her and smile.

"What?," she asked. "Would you like to dance?," he asked in response.

"I would love to," Kiera said with a huge smile. Mason got up and took her hand.

Placing his hand in the small of her back, he escorted her to the dance floor. Once there he spun her into his arms and dipped her. She felt as if she was in a fairy tale. Mason loved how her body felt against his. He pulled her closer. Kiera loved the scent of his cologne. She laid her head on his chest.

Suddenly she felt the vibrations. When she looked up, Mason was singing. They were so wrapped up in each other that they didn't notice that the music stopped. Mason kept singing as he looked into her eyes. She couldn't believe he was actually singing to her. Then it happened. Kiera grabbed his head and kissed him.

Mason was shocked but loved the feeling of her lips. They were soft. Kiera was embarrassed but wanted to do it again. She had never been so daring. Mason pulled her closer. Leaning in he kissed her back.

He gently sucked on her bottom lip. She opened her mouth, releasing sounds of passion. He slid his tongue inside her mouth. She moaned as she grinded her body against his. Their bodies hungered for each other's. She felt his manhood throbbing between them.

"Ahem, excuse me Mason and Kiera," a voice said from somewhere nearby. They stopped kissing to see where the voice came from. Geraldo stood mere inches away. The room was packed. Bodies were undulating to the music. Mason and Kiera felt embarrassed. Some of couples stood watching them.

"Sorry Mason. I've been trying to get your attention. Your foods has been ready for ten minutes. I've been keeping it hot. If you would like, I'll bring it out now," Geraldo said.

"It's okay," Mason responded as he escorted Kiera back off the dance floor.

When they got back to their table they noticed it roped off. A big muscular man stood just outside the rope. The man turned everyone away that attempted to sit there. Smiling, he pulled back the rope when he saw Kiera and Mason approaching.

"Hey Mack how's everything going?," Mason asked once they got closer.

"I'm doing great Mason. I would ask you the same but if that pretty woman is any indication then, I know your doing a lot better than me," Mack responded.

"She is amazingly beautiful, isn't she?," Mason said staring into her eyes. His thumb circled the small of her back.

97

Kiera couldn't help but blush. She definitely wanted to be his girlfriend, maybe more. She noticed Mason made no attempt to correct the assumption. She couldn't help but wonder how he felt about her.

Mason led Kiera past the ropes and to their table. Mack closed the rope behind them. The other patrons watched from a distance. Mack stood guard to ensure that Mason and Kiera weren't disturbed.

Once again, Mason pulled out her chair. By now their stomachs were growling. Just as Mason went to sit down, Geraldo showed up with dinner.

The meal consisted of Balsamic chicken breasts, rice pilaf, sweet potatoes with marshmallows and steamed seasonal vegetables. It was love at first bite. Dinner was mouthwatering delicious. In between bites they talked. As hungry as they were, they were interested more in each other.

"Excuse me Mason but I need to use the ladies room," Kiera said as she got up from the table. Mason stood up and pulled out her seat. He couldn't help but watch as she walked away. It seemed all eyes were on the two of them.

Although, she only had two glasses Kiera struggled to walk straight. Her face was flushed and her panties were drenched. Kiera rushed inside as soon as she saw the sign for the bathroom. She walked over to the sink and wet her face. She couldn't believe what happened. No man had ever been able to touch her, kiss her or talk to her and make her orgasm until now. She wanted Mason badly.

Suddenly, she heard voices outside. Feeling embarrassed about the effect Mason had on her Kiera ducked into the bathroom stall. She felt foolish but didn't want anyone to see her. She listened as two women entered the bathroom.

"Girl this place is kind of lame tonight. From what I'm seen most of the fine men are married. The single ones are out of shape or positively ugly," Kiera heard one of them say.

"You ain't never lied. There is that one guy at that roped off table. Now he is definitely fine. Give me your lipstick so I can write my number down," the other woman said.

"Stacy he's here with another woman," her friend said laughing. She then passed her the lipstick.

"Yeah Tia I know. He should be here with me. There's no way, that woman can handle a man like him. I guarantee you I'll have that man eating out the palm of my hand and so hooked he'll buy me anything I want," Stacy replied.

The two women laughed. Inside the stall Kiera was boiling hot. She listened as the two women gave each other a high five and walked out the bathroom. Kiera walked out of the stall. She want to storm after them and beat them till they were black and blue. Although she was just to know Mason she felt he was different.

How dare these women plot to get her man? Why couldn't they find a man of their own? Kiera stood for a while trying to think of what to do. Whatever she did, she knew she wasn't going to lose him without a fight.

Just then she heard the beat to one of her favorite songs. R. Kelly's "Move Your Body Like A Snake" was blaring through the speakers. She knew exactly what she was going to do. She stepped back into the stall letting the door shut behind her. Once inside, Kiera hiked up her skirt and slid her boy shorts off.

A quick thrill overcame her. With her boy shorts balled up in her hand, Kiera walked out the bathroom. She wasn't sure if it was her or the alcohol but she had new found confidence.

Her hips swayed with every step. Mason stood as he saw her quickly approaching. Something was definitely different. Gone was the nervousness and shyness. There was purpose in her stride. Every man in the room was looking.

She walked up and placed a passionate kiss on Mason's lips. Her tongue now explored his mouth. Her hand caressed his muscular chest as she placed her boy shorts in his jacket pocket.

Mason was so enthralled with her that he didn't notice. His manhood throbbed against her. Their bodies burned with desire for one another. His hands slid down her back, resting on her firm buttocks. Suddenly, Kiera broke the kiss and began to whisper in his ear, "Dance with me!"

Mason took off his jacket and placed it over the back of the chair. As if in a trance, he followed her to the dance floor. Kiera looked around the room. Uncertain what the women from the bathroom looked like, she decided to make sure every woman there knew Mason was hers.

Kiera began swaying her cobra like hips. She reached up behind her and pulled Mason's head down. He kissed along the nape of her neck and nibbled on her ear. Since she had no panties on, Kiera felt every inch of his manhood pulsating against her buttocks.

Mason loved how she felt so much that he never noticed the song ended. Mason found himself holding her a little longer. Suddenly, his ribs started aching. He clinched his teeth and smiled. He didn't want to ruin the moment.

"Baby are you alright?," Kiera asked. "Just hurting a little," Mason replied.

Kiera grabbed his hand. This time she led him back to the table. She could tell from the way he paused between words, that he was attempting to catch his breath. As soon as Mack saw them coming back to the table, he quickly cleared the area. He could tell something was wrong. He pulled out a chair for Mason and then disappeared into the kitchen. Kiera started tending to Mason. Seconds later, Mack returned with Geraldo in tow.

"Mason are you alright?," both men asked simultaneously.

"Yeah, just a little winded," Mason answered clutching his side.

"Winded," both men uttered in unison.

"Are you sure that pretty little lady isn't wearing you out old man?," Geraldo asked jokingly.

Clutching his ribs, Mason laughed. Mason stopped to look at Kiera. A look of guilt and concern was written all over her face. The moment she realized he was looking, she buried her face in her hands.

"Kiera!," Mason said as he called out to her.

She raised her head slowly. Tears streamed down her beautiful face. Mason hated seeing her cry. He pulled her chair closer to him. She looked at him briefly before letting her gaze fall back down to the floor.

Mason placed his hand under her chin and slowly raised her head. He looked into her sultry eyes. He watched as the light seemed to dance inside them. Her bottom lip was quivering.

101

Mason leaned in closer. He took Kiera's bottom lip between his. Their tongues explored each other's mouth.

"Let's get out of here," Mason whispered in her ear. The words sent shock waves of erotic ecstasy shooting down her spine. She nodded in agreement. Mason grabbed his jacket and they began to leave.

"Hey Mason, you sure you don't need to go to the hospital?," Geraldo inquired.

"No need. She's a nurse," Mason said taking Kiera' s hand in his.

"Well let me know if she's got any single friends that are nurses. I definitely could use some TLC myself," Geraldo said smiling as he gave them both a hug.

Mason grabbed a tight hold of Kiera. He realized they had walk through the crowd. R. Kelly's "Bump and Grind" started playing. That's exactly what they were all doing. As they walked someone struck Mason in the side. He doubled over in pain. He loosened his grip just enough that Kiera and him managed to get separated. Kiera found her blocked behind a wall of men. Each one dancing and trying to get her attention.

"Kiera!," a voice shouted from somewhere behind her.

She whirled around excitedly hoping to see Mason. When she turned around she thought she had seen a ghost. The man smiled back at her flashing his gold tooth. Her past had found her. She was scared to death and needed to get out of there. She looked around. "Where's Mason?," she nervously asked herself.

"Hey Kiera, I thought that was you," the man said as he stepped closer.

"Hi Marcus," Kiera replied.

She began to step back in an effort to create some distance. Marcus smiled and tried to grab her. She screamed. Hearing her, Mason looked around feverishly. Despite his efforts he didn't see her. His heart began racing. Adrenaline now replaced and quieted the pain he once felt.

Marcus stood there looking around. The music was so loud that nobody stopped to help her. Realizing that, he attempted to grab her again. Kiera screamed once more. "How did they find her?," was the question that popped inside her head. She then balled up in the fetal position and closed her eyes.

"Kiera my love, are you alright?," she heard a somewhat familiar voice say.

She slowly opened her eyes. She was afraid Marcus would still be standing over her, watching and waiting. She also was afraid she would awake from a dream and be back in the arms of someone far worse. When she finally looked up, there stood her knight in shining armor. Mason stood there with his hand extended.

Kiera immediately jumped into his arms. For the first time in her life she felt safe. It was at that moment she realized the music had stopped. Mack and Geraldo stood closely behind Mason. Everyone seemed to be looking at her.

"Baby are you alright?," Mason asked for a second time.

Kiera wasn't certain exactly when she became his baby but, she loved how it sound. She scanned the room, looking at every face. None of them resembled Marcus. He had vanished. Kiera laughed. She wondered if he was ever truly there. Maybe it was just the alcohol.

"I'm fine Mason. Let's just get out of here," Kiera told him.

Mason took her hand in his once more. With his other hand, he smoothed the hair back behind her ear. She couldn't help but wonder where this man had been all her life. She was on cloud nine. Suddenly Mason opened his hand.

"Here baby," Mason said as he handed her a piece of paper.

"What's this?," she questioned. Mason merely shrugged his shoulders. Now confused Kiera opened it. The name Stacy was written inside along with a number. It was all written in red lipstick. The woman that gave it to him even went as far as to place a kiss on it.

"Where did you get this from?," Kiera asked, trying to mask her anger. "The light skin woman by the bar," Mason replied. Kiera looked behind him towards the bar. The area around it was crowded. Patrons stood around talking and ordering drinks. Women stood around waiting for men to buy them drinks.

"Which one?," she inquired.

"The slender woman in the blue dress and black pumps on. She has long curly hair past her shoulders. She's talking to a short dark skinned woman in a black dress," he responded.

He never turned once to look behind him. Kiera slowly scanned the area until her eyes fell on a slim, leggy woman in a tight blue dress. She was beautiful. Thoughts began to run wild in Kiera's head. She didn't think she was attractive enough to compete with the woman.

When she looked up, she noticed the woman looking in their direction. She was staring directly at Kiera. Suddenly, the woman waved.

After that, Stacy tapped her friend. They both pointed and laughed. Kiera had never felt so disrespected by another woman. Win or lose, she was ready to fight. She tried to move around Mason. She knew she would have to fight them both but didn't care. Mason stepped in her way with every attempt.

The alcohol she had drank earlier only fueled her rage. Mack and Geraldo joined in to block her path. The whole time the women taunted her and laughed. Kiera was enraged. She couldn't understand why Mason was stopping her. Did he want her ? He was able to describe her completely without a second look. Everyone was looking at her.

She saw a tall muscular well built man and she knew exactly how to have the last laugh. She would make Mason jealous. Fixing her dress, she began a slow seductive walk in direction. He was sipping on a beer and wouldn't take his eyes off of her. A smile was plastered on his face. Kiera smiled back as she stopped in front of him. Kiera turned and looked at Mason. He stood watching and shaking his head. He looked more hurt than jealous.

Shrugging his shoulders, Mason turned to walk off. Kiera was almost certain he was going to walk over to Stacy and her friend. She stood there shocked when instead he headed for the front door. She stood there baffled. Mason was different. He was the type of man she prayed for. She felt just as trashy as the women that were still watching her.

When she turned back around the man was ogling her. The way he was licking his lips made her feel uncomfortable. Her skin started to crawl. It reminded her of every man she had ever encountered in her past. She felt like meat. Mason made her feel like a Queen.

"Can I buy you a drink Miss?," the man asked.

"Um no thank you. I have to go," she replied.

"Well maybe, we can get together later and have some fun. Can I get your number?," the man asked.

Kiera looked down at her hand. She was still holding the paper Mason gave her. As angry and tempted as she was to give him the paper, she decided not to. She couldn't put a finger on it but she felt a eerily creepy feeling about him. Kiera spun around on her heels and went to find Mason.

The stranger watched as she walked away. His temper was flaring. He wanted to go after her but, he had watched her long enough to know she wasn't alone. He vowed that they would meet again.

Kiera could feel Stacy and her friend watching her. With every step she began ripping the paper with Stacy's number. When she felt all the pieces were small enough, she threw them in the air. She then whirled around as the confetti fell around her.

She found Mason waiting for the elevator. She rushed into his arms. She wanted everyone there to know he was her man. Placing a hand on his chest and wrapping the other around his neck, she kissed him. Instantly, she noticed something was wrong.

106

Something was different. Mason was that man she had wanted for months. She never believed he would even look her way. She wanted to jump for joy when he asked her out. Now after getting to know him she wanted something real and lasting with him. She attempted to kiss him once more.

"Let's go," Mason ordered as he gently pushed her away and got on the elevator. Kiera immediately began apologizing as the doors closed.

"Not now," he said and then rode up in silence.

"The strong, silent, take charge type," she thought to herself. Mason was a handsome, intellectual, respectful and even humorous man. He also had a tough, strong and assertive side. She found all those features to be quite sexy in a man. Those were the traits she looked for in a husband.

As soon as they stepped outside the valet rushed off to retrieve Mason's car. The temperature must have dropped while they were inside. Mason looked over and noticed Kiera was trembling. The crisp night air cut down to the very bone.

"Kiera you're cold," Mason said. He took off his jacket and placed it around her shoulders. Kiera stepped into his arms. He could smell the scent of her hair. He rubbed her arms trying to warm her up.

"Look Kiera, I think we need to talk," Mason suddenly said.

"Mason I am sorry. I know my behavior was uncalled for. I don't know what came over me. Maybe I shouldn't drink....," Kiera was rattling on.

"Kiera please let me speak," Mason interjected.

"I'm sorry," she said apologetically.

"Can you do me one favor though? Please tell me why you got jealous and was ready to fight in there?," he asked.

"Mason she was a beautiful woman. I can't even compete with her. To be honest I kept asking myself all night why are you here with me? I understand if you wanted to let me down slowly," Kiera said with tears welling up in her eyes.

"Kiera what are you talking about? The whole time we were in there every man in the place was trying to get your attention. As hurt as I am I would have fought every one of them. You are beautiful, intelligent, sensitive and more. Every woman in there paled in comparison to you. I gave you the paper to let you know, I am not trying to play or run game. I want and need something real and forever. Why do you feel that you are ugly?," Mason said.

"Baby I'm so sorry. I don't know why I acted the way I did", she responded. Mason could see the pain in her eyes. Kiera was definitely hurting. He wanted to hold her. It wanted to promise her forever but it was too soon.

"I sure hope the valet comes back soon. It is getting a little cold out here," Mason said trying to change the conversation.

"Mason you're going to get sick," Kiera said. She tried to give him his jacket back.

"No Kiera besides, I highly doubt that I'll get sick being out here for a little bit without a jacket. My body stays hot. If I do get sick though, it'll give me a chance to spend time with this real sexy nurse that I sort of have eyes for," he said brushing the hair out of her face.

"Oh is that so Mr. Mason?," she said smiling.

108

"It most certainly is Ms. Williams," Mason responded with a smirk of his own.

Placing his hand under her chin, Mason leaned in to kiss her. He immediately ignited her flames of passion. Her heart started beating like drums. She found it hard to breathe. She wanted his lips on every inch of her body. She wanted to feel him deep inside her.

Beep, beep They were startled by the sound of a blaring car horn. When they looked around, the valet had pulled up in Mason's car. The valet sat there just staring and smiling. When she noticed how he was staring, she began to blush. She felt a little embarrassed.

Taking slow, confident strides, Mason opened the passenger side door. He made sure she was comfortable and secured in her seat before, walking to the driver's side. Just as Mason reached for the handle the valet hopped out.

He stood there looking at Mason. His hand was extended as he stood there smiling. Mason quickly dug his hand into his pocket. He pulled out a hundred dollars and handed to the valet.

"Thank you Mr. Steele. Please drive safely and have a good night," the valet said. Stuffing the money into his pocket, the valet rushed off to get another car.

Mason shook his head and then got in the car. He put on his seatbelt, adjusted the mirrors, and started the engine. Just before he drove off, Mason turned and looked at Kiera. She was staring back and smiling.

"Such a beautiful smile. What did I possibly do to deserve it?," he asked.

"In the small time that we have known each other you continue to surprise me. You genuinely care about people," she replied.

"Kiera I'm nobody special. I am no different from any other man," he told her.

Kiera had known many men in her past. Mason was different. He has a way of making everyone he meets feel important. She was impressed. She wanted to know more about him.

"Do you mind if I ask, what made you give the valet a hundred dollars? See if I hadn't watched how you've interacted with people since we met, I would have thought it was some wild trick to impress me," she said to him.

"Well did it work?," Mason asked jokingly.

"If you're lucky perhaps, you'll find out the answer to that later on," Kiera replied seductively.

Mason smiled. He sat there speechless. Meanwhile, in his mind he welcomed the thought of being inside her. His body hungered for her but he needed something real. She seemed to have everything he was looking for in a woman. Time would tell. The hunger in his flesh was wrestling with the desire of his heart. He didn't want to ruin this with meaningless sex.

"Mason? Are you alright?," she questioned.

"Umm...", he said clearing his throat. "Oh yeah, I'm fine, why?"

"You never answered my question. "Why did you give the valet a hundred dollars?," she asked once more.

G "Oh Everett! He was homeless. Everyone he ever loved and cared about was murdered," Mason finally answered.

"What? When? How?," she asked. She sat in suspense.

"Like I said, they were murdered. It was about three years ago, Everett ran around with this gang. Actually the same gang we had a run in with before. Well this gang executed a member of a rival gang. It just so happened their War Chief decided to leave the gang earlier that morning." "The gang felt betrayed and knew he had to much information on them. When they were questioned on the murder, they named Everett as the shooter. The police found him and picked him up while he waited for his wife outside of a family health clinic. Word got to the rival gang. They shot her as she walked out. She was pregnant. Doctors tried to save the baby but it was too late." "Police found his mother raped and murdered in an alley. Her body was laying on a pile of trash like she was garbage. She was one block from home. Everett's dad was one of my closest friends. When he found out, he snapped. It was too much for him. He hung himself." "When police found out who really did the shooting they released him. The landlord where he lived was frightened. He didn't want any trouble so, he kicked Everett out into the streets. Right now he works and goes to school. He is trying to become a lawyer because he wants to take the gangs off the streets. He wants to be someone his parents, wife and kid would have been proud of," Mason informed her.

Kiera sat in awe. She watched as Everett drove up in another car, hopped out and rushed off to get the next. He worked diligently. From the smile he had plastered out his face, she never would've known he had been through so much. Mason backed up and pulled out into traffic. Everett waved. Mason honked back in response. The night air felt liberating as they drove away.

Chapter 22

Somewhere across town the white van pulled into a seemingly deserted warehouse. Snipers lie in wait. The mysterious man turned off the engine and reached for the camera. All eyes and guns were focused on him.

The man desperately wanted to see what was on the camera. He was tempted to sit in the van and start going through it. Outside was quiet. Too quiet. He reached for his radio." T-Rex , it's Cam! Stand down!!," he shouted over the radio.

Cam sat back awaiting a response. None came. Still he waited. After five minutes, he was slowly starting to grow impatient. He knew if he stepped out of the van, he was a dead man. T-Rex was the only man he trusted and one of a few people who ever saw his real face.

Suddenly, there was two knocks on the door. The man peeked out the window. T-Rex now stood outside. He was holding a briefcase. The man slid the door open.

"Hey T-Rex did anything happen while I was away?," he asked as he reached for the briefcase.

"Naw, it's been quiet. Too quiet if you ask me. How'd everything work out Chameleon?," T-Rex asked.

After a few minutes, Chameleon stepped out of the van. His badly scarred face now concealed. "Well I got the camera. I'll see if anything important is on it. Meet me in the office in an hour," Chameleon instructed before walking away.

T-Rex turned and walked back toward the gym. Chameleon strutted to his office with confidence. His men feared him. He smirked. The toughest gang of thugs, hitmen and murderers and they all feared and worked for him. He loved the thought of that.

Reaching his office, Chameleon punched in his access code. He heard the all too familiar double beep and unlocking sound of the door. Easing the door open slightly, he slipped inside. He gently closed the door behind him. The lights automatically turned on as he made his way over to his desk.

Chameleon placed the camera on the desk. He then poured himself a glass of White Hennessey, that he picked while in Jamaica. He took a sip and sat down. It was just what he needed.

He stared at the camera in front of him. He dreamt of taking everything Mason ever worked for. He wanted to take everything and everyone from him. He wanted to watch him suffer. After that, he would take the only thing Mr. Mason Steele had left...his life.

 Taking the digital camera in his hands, he scrolled through the pictures. He wanted to make sure he missed nothing. He scanned each picture for five minutes. He looked for the smallest detail. Not finding anything worthwhile, he grew more and more infuriated. Suddenly, he saw something or better yet someone.

In the picture was a shapely woman who appeared to be leaving Mason's apartment. That picture may prove to be important. The way it was taken made it virtually impossible to make her face. Whoever she was, her figure was remarkable.

Chameleon sat there wondering who she was. Somehow she was important to Mason Steele. That made her important to him. Intel never mentioned any woman. He needed to find her. Perhaps, she was just what he needed to take down Mason Steele. A smile crept across his face. Just then, the office door swung open.

"Ah, just the man I was waiting on. Come in!," Chameleon said as he got up to pour another drink. He knew Tre was the only other person with an access code to his office. Tre walked in and closed the door behind him.

"Join me in a drink. Let's celebrate," Chameleon said as he passed T-Rex a glass.

"Why? Did you find what we needed?, " Tre asked as he pulled out a chair and slumped down in it.

"Not exactly!," Chameleon replied. "However, we may have found our bargaining chip."

Tre immediately sat up in the chair. He looked like a child awaiting a gift on Christmas day. Chameleon had his complete attention. Knowing that Chameleon passed him the camera. Tre did just as Chameleon had done. He scrolled through the pictures. He stopped on the picture of the mysterious woman.

"Who is she and how can we find her?", Tre asked and continued talking, " "Looking at this picture we can't exactly see her face".

"That's your job. Use your men and find her. Find out who she is. We can negotiate her release in exchange for the "Keeper project." Once we get our hands on the project, kill her. Make sure Mason Steele watches her die," Chameleon instructed.

Tre kept staring at the picture. Something bothered him about it. Although he couldn't make out her face, something about her looked all too familiar. He tried to shake thought out his head.

"It's impossible," he whispered to himself. For three years, he had searched for the love of his life. She simply disappeared. She couldn't be the woman in the pictures.

Suddenly, there was a knock at the door. "Who is it?," Tre asked.

"Yo, Tee! It's me, Marcus," a voice answered from the hallway.

"Come in!," Tre ordered. He immediately recognized the voice. It belonged to his most loyal soldier and best friend.

"Man, you won't believe who I just saw..." Marcus started rattling off as he opened the door.

"Who did you see?," Chameleon asked.

"Oh I'm s-s-s-so s-s-s-sorry Chameleon sir, I d-d-didn't know you were back," Marcus stuttered. He had known Chameleon just as long as Tre had but being around him always made Marcus nervous.

"It's quite alright Marcus. Just relax and tell us who you saw," Chameleon said calmly.

Marcus took a deep breath before blurting out his answer rather excitedly, "Tre I saw her."

"Who did you see?," Tre asked. Both he and Chameleon sat in up their chairs.

"Kiera, Tre ! I saw Kiera!!," Marcus shouted as if he had won the lottery.

Just the mere mention if her name made Tre jump right out of his seat. "Could it be?," he thought to himself.

115

He had all but given up on finding her. Staring intensely at Marcus, Tre grabbed him by the collar. "Where did you see her? Are you sure it was her? Who was she with?," Tre asked as he continued to rattle off a barrage of questions.

"Well I was at Geraldo's with this woman I had just met. Anyway when I looked up there she was. I wasn't sure it was her at first. I got up and got a closer look. The moment our eyes connected her expression changed. She called my name and screamed. The guy that the gang beat up in the alley came to her side so, I hightailed it out of there," Marcus told them.

Tre reached into his pocket. He pulled out his cellphone and car keys. "Marcus come on. I need you to show me exactly where you saw her," he said excitedly as he headed for the door. Chameleon sat back in his chair laughing. He picked up the camera and looked at the picture. "Could it possibly be?," he thought to himself as he laughed even harder. His sounds of laughter infuriated Tre and stopped him in his tracks.

Tre was prepared to say something but, Chameleon was the only man Tre feared and respected so, he chose his words carefully. "What's wrong boss?," Tre asked.

"Where are you rushing off to?," Chameleon asked.

"I'm going to take Marcus and head over to Geraldo's. Did you need me for anything before I leave?" Tre asked although deep down inside he was ready to go.

"That can wait until tomorrow," Chameleon said calmly as he sat back in his chair, tapping the camera.

116

"No offense Chameleon but, what do you mean that it can hold until tomorrow?," Tre asked. He was boiling inside.

"Well, I am looking at this picture here and if she is the same woman it will be great. I listened to Marcus and Mason Steele must be attracted to her. You might not like what I am about to say but, maybe we should let him fall in love with her. Maybe if watch and follow them, we can get our hands on the "Keeper Project," he said calmly.

Tre didn't want to hear that. He wanted to find Kiera. She was his and he couldn't bear the thought of her in another man's arms. Now he was being asked to let another man fall in love with her. Chameleon wanted him to sit back and watch his childhood enemy and his wife fall in love with each other. Sure it would help them but Tre still didn't like the idea.

"What are you suggesting?," Tre asked through clenched teeth.

Chameleon got up and retrieved another glass. He then walked over to his liquor cabinet. He pulled out his Johnny Walker Scotch and poured them drinks. "First thing I suggest is that we all sit down and have a drink," he said as he pointed to the two chairs in front of his desk. He was excited. It was a time to celebrate.

Tre and Marcus looked at one another and then sat down. They knew his were more an order than a suggestion Chameleon walked over and gave them both a drink. Grabbing his own glass he sat down. "Gentleman, we've found just what we need to not only destroy Mason Steele but also get our hands on plans to destroy the government's military, he said as he sat back smiling.

Putting on a half smile Tre took a sip. His mind was on finding Kiera and getting her back. Nothing else mattered. He sat back devising a plan on how to make it happen. For now, he would do just as Chameleon suggested. He would watch her. The moment opportunity struck he would get her back. "Tomorrow is a new day," he thought to himself and smiled.

Chapter 23

The drive home took mere minutes. The roads were
practically empty. Mason pulled his car into the parking
garage and hopped out to open Kiera's. She took his hand
smiling as she got out of the car. She felt like a Queen.

All the way back home Mason stared at Kiera's legs
again. They were smooth, thick and incredibly sexy. She was
teasing him by rubbing her legs together and resting her
hand on his knee. He imagined them wrapped around his waist.

He also watched the rise and fall of her breasts as she
breathed. He would smile as she ran her fingers through her
hair. His breathing got heavy when she licked her lips. When
she looked at him, he wanted to take her right there in the
car.

Kiera was amazing. Mason couldn't deny his attraction
for her. She seemed like the type of woman he always wanted
but he knew she had been hurt. He understood her pain and
knew she needed something real. Tonight was the first time,
he actually enjoyed the company of a woman.

The wind was blowing hard. Kiera was shivering as they
walked. Pulling her close, Mason wrapped his arms around
her. He never wanted to let her go.
Mason pushed the button for the elevator. As they waited
Kiera stepped closer. Mason looked into her as she smiled.
She got closer still. Seconds later they were kissing. The
moment broken only by the ding of the elevator.

Mason stepped to the side to allow her on. Kiera
brushed her hand down his arm as she got on. Taking her
hand, he stepped inside. The doors closed behind him.
Mason pressed the button for her floor.

When he turned to look at her, she smiled and shook her finger at him. Mason laughed. He didn't want the date to end. Kiera stood there, a bit confused. She wanted to feel him inside her. She wanted the comfort of his company. She wanted the safety of his arms.

The elevator slowly ascended. Mason pulled her close once more. His tongue explored hers. His hands caressed her curves. She moaned. As the elevator passed he floor, Mason found himself peeking at the doors. He was afraid they would be have company.

Suddenly the elevator stopped. The doors opened. Mason pushed himself away. Kiera looked at him laughing. They were so locked up in their kiss that she had accidentally pressed the button. Mason looked out the doors. No one was there. The doors closed as he steeped back in. When he turned around Kiera was snickering.

"What are you laughing about?," Mason asked.

"Oh nothing," she replied.

"Did you push that button?," he asked.

"I don't know what you're talking about. You should've seen yourself though. You looked like a scared little high school kid," she told him as she giggled uncontrollably.

"Really?," he inquired.

"You sure was," she said still laughing.

"Mmm don't make me spank you, " Mason said jokingly.

Instead of Kiera being scared, she turned around. Looking over her shoulder she hiked up her skirt and flashed him. For the first time Mason realized she had no panties on. He looked around as if someone else was watching.

"Spank me," she said seductively. Mason stepped forward until he was directly behind her. Feeling him behind her, Kiera began grinding her butt on his manhood. It immediately sprang to life. The material stretching. He wanted her desperately.

He kissed the nape of her neck. She moaned. Her nipples were hard. She could feel him against. She needed him inside her. Suddenly, they heard the final ding.

Straightening her clothes quickly, they laughed as the doors opened. They stepped out and headed down the hall. Kiera's apartment was close by. Reaching in her bag Kiera pulled out her keys. Mason held her waist as she opened the door. She turned around and kissed him.

Their kiss grew passionate. The door flew opened as they leaned against it. Never once breaking the kiss, Mason picked her up and carried her inside. Mason pushed the door closed with his foot. The fires of passion burned inside them. They stumbled as they embraced. Falling onto the couch they laughed.

"Take me Mason, " Kiera moaned.

Mason took off his jacket. Mason kissed down her neck. She ripped his shirt open and started kissing on his chest. He ran his hands down her legs. He wanted her now. Conflicted

he stopped. He knew this was wrong. He didn't want this to be another meaningless relationship. He needed something more. He needed something real.

Stopping Mason stood up. He looked down at Kiera. He couldn't believe he was about to do what he was going to do. Putting his jacket back on, he straightened his clothes and then headed for the door. "Where are you going?," Kiera asked.

"I've got to go," Mason said as he reached for the door knob.

"Why? What's wrong? ," Kiera asked somewhat confused as to why he was leaving.

"Everything's alright Kiera. I just don't think we should do this," he said as he opened the door.

Mason turned to look at Kiera. She was still lying on the couch. He was tempted to join her. Deciding that wouldn't be best, Mason stepped into the hallway closing the door behind him. Kiera jumped off the couch and raced to the door. When she opened the door he was gone. She stepped in the hallway only to hear the elevator doors closing. Now feeling rejected and angry Kiera stepped back into her apartment slamming the door shut.

Mason paced back and forth in the elevator. He kicked the elevator wall. He couldn't believe he walked away. Kiera was an amazing woman. She seemed to possess all the qualities he longed for in a woman. He couldn't help but wonder if he had made the right decision.

The elevator doors opened and Mason stepped into the lobby. A group of people were walking in talking and laughing. There were also couples coming in from dinner and a movie. He watched as women held on to their men. Men catered to their women's every need. They were happy and in love.

As he stepped into the crisp night air he knew he had made the right choice. He still yearned to go back but, he wanted more in his life. Every since Johnny and his wife were expecting children something in Mason changed. He was tired of being alone. He wanted a family of his own and the love of a good woman.

Mason stepped into the lobby of his apartment building. He turned his attention to the front desk. Dexter wasn't there. Mason walked over to the office door and knocked. No one answered. Something was wrong. Dexter would never abandon his post.

Recalling how nervous and secretive Dexter had looked earlier made Mason feel guilty. Perhaps he should have stayed with him. He waited an hour but Dexter never showed up. Mason couldn't help but feel concerned and a little responsible.

He walked behind the front desk. When he got back there he was greeted by a mess. Empty bottles of water and soda were lined up. He found gum wrappers with some containing chewed up pieces of gum. He also found a bowl of salad. The lettuce was already brown inside. The garbage was overflowing. Suddenly Mason noticed a half eaten bowl of lasagna. Dexter loved lasagna and would never leave any behind.

Mason wanted to call the management office but knew they were already closed for the evening. Mason cleaned up what he could and placed the trash in the dumpster outside. Placing the lasagna in the mini fridge, Mason continued to worry. He looked at the clock that sat on the desk. It was twelve o'clock midnight.

Mason pulled out his cellphone and called Dexter's phone. He figured nobody would answer but he needed to know everything was alright. The phone rang and rang. The phone went to voicemail. He tried again. Nobody picked up so Mason left a voice message.

Realizing it was getting late, Mason decided to call it a night. His ribs started hurting once more. Clutching his side, Mason slowly lumbered over to the elevator. The doors opened and he stepped inside. He pressed the button for his floor and watched as the doors closed.

He was alone. His mind immediately went to Kiera with her skirt hiked up around her waist. He remembered the softness of her skin, the swell of her breasts and her intoxicating scent. Mason stepped off the elevator laughing. There was definitely something special about Kiera. She was affecting him in a way that no other woman had. Just the mere thought of her made his body hunger for her. He couldn't get her out of his mind.

By the time Mason reached his apartment the pain was unbearable. He entered the apartment feeling as if he would pass out from the pain. Mason pulled his jacket off and tossed it on the couch. Staggering he rushed into the kitchen. He was shaking uncontrollably.

Mason searched around feverishly until he found his medication. Turning on the faucet he gulped it down and tossed the cup in the sink. His eyes were tearing up as he tried to bite back the pain. Mason collapsed in his favorite chair. He laid his head back and closed his eyes. Slowly the pain started to subside.

He opened his eyes as he tried to focus. Something black lie crumpled up on the floor by his jacket. Sliding up in his seat Mason reached down and picked it up. It was a pair of lace panties. They were Kiera's. He thought back to the elevator. She must have slipped them into his jacket but he couldn't figure out when. Just then he remembered something.

He got into the apartment but never unlocked the door. He remembered watching as Kiera locked the door. Somebody must have been there after they left. Now feeling groggy Mason pushed himself out of the chair and staggered to the door. Once there he checked the door jamb. It hadn't been forced in. Either Kiera thought she locked the door or someone came in with a key.

Still feeling out of it Mason did the best he could to make sure nothing was stolen. After thirty minutes of staggering through the apartment, Mason determined nothing was stolen. He grabbed his keys and fumbled with the lock. Once he was certain the lock worked, he locked the door and went back to sit down.

The medication was starting to work. Mason looked down at his hand. He was still clutching on to Kiera's panties. He wanted to call her and explain why he left. He also wanted to apologize. He felt he owed her that.

Sitting up, he pulled the phone out his pants pocket. He could feel his eyes getting heavy. He always had a low tolerance for medicine. Trying to fight back the oncoming sleep, he scrolled through his cellphone in search of her number. Yawning he found it. He thought of everything he wanted to say as he started to press the call button.

Chapter 24

Beep beep, beep beep, beep beep. Mason jumped up. He was startled out of his sleep. Sunlight shined through the window. Mason looked for his phone and found it lying on the floor. Mason picked it up and turned off the alarm.

Looking at the time, he was shocked. It was eleven thirty in the morning. He looked for Kiera's number once more. Locating it, he called her. The phone rang repeatedly. No one answered.

All sorts of thoughts ran through his head. He couldn't help but feel she was ignoring his call. Hanging up the phone Mason went to make himself something to eat. The whole time he knew he had to figure out a way to get closer to Kiera.

After eating, Mason took off the bandages and went to take a shower. He figured it was better to explain in person. When he stepped in the shower the water felt rejuvenating. As he went to dry off , he walked into her bedroom. He could see movement and rapidly got dressed.

Grabbing his wallet and keys Mason headed for the door. He locked the door and made sure it was locked before heading for the elevator. He didn't have to wait long before it arrived. He got on and watched the doors close behind him.

The whole ride down to the lobby images of Kiera popped into his head. He knew that he not only needed to apologize but he wanted to do something special for her. He thought long and hard. Suddenly, he thought of just the thing.

As soon as the elevator reached the lobby and the doors opened, Mason quickly started to walk towards the door. Something or should he say someone caught his attention out of the corner of his eye. He immediately stopped in his tracks. He turned and made a beeline for the front desk.

"Hey Ralph, how's it been? I haven't seen you in quite sometime," Mason said as he approached the front desk.

"Hi Mr. Steele. Everything is great. I moved up to management. How have you been?," he asked in return.

"Everything is going perfectly well. Look Ralph, I know you are busy but do you mind if I ask you a question?," Mason said.

"What would you like to know Mr. Steele?," he asked.

"I was just wondering if Mr. Turner was alright?," Mason inquired.

"Dexter called in late last night. He said he needed to go home. He had an emergency situation and may be out for a few weeks. Apparently his mother's ill," Ralph informed him.

"Thanks Ralph," Mason said as he headed for the door.

Mason reached for his phone. If what Ralph said is true then it must be really serious. From what Mason could remember Dexter and his mom had somewhat of a strained relationship. The phone rang and rang.

As Mason walked out the door, he tried again. He got the same results. He decided to leave a voicemail and put his phone in his pocket. Just as Mason reached for the door handle to the neighboring building, a cab pulls up. Mason turns to see Kiera sitting in the back.

He leans against the wall watching as she gets out. He stands still in awe of her beauty. She reaches into her purse so that she can pay the driver. Realizing that she either hasn't noticed him or is choosing to ignore him, Mason walks up behind her.

"How much is it sir?," Mason asks the cab driver.

"That'll be seven dollars sir," the cab driver replies.

Mason reached into his pocket and paid the driver.
Kiera still didn't look up. He knows that she is definitely
ignoring him. "She must really be mad about last night,"
Mason thought to himself.

"Thank you sir, but I assure you I can afford to pay my
fare on my own Mr. Steele," Kiera says suddenly. When he
looked at her she was standing there with her arm extended
and holding out seven dollars.

"Kiera baby stop," Mason pleads.

"Oh now you want to talk," she says angrily.

The cab driver sat watching. He watched as she started to
cry. Mason reached for her. She pulled away and shouted
angrily. The cab driver got out to defend her. "Is there a
problem ma'am?," the driver asked.

Kiera stood there sobbing. She really liked Mason. He
made her feel as if she wasn't good enough. She hated how
she practically threw herself at him last night only to be
rejected.

"Everything is fine sir," Mason says trying to diffuse
the situation before it escalated.

"It's alright sir," Kiera told the driver as she saw
him reaching for a baseball bat.

"Are you sure ma'am?," the driver asked as he pointed
the bat at Mason.

"Yes I am sir and thank you," she answered as she gave
him a tip and closed the door.

Mason could see how hurt she was. Kiera was struggling hard not to cry. Mason wanted to hold and comfort her. She pushed past him as she walked to the building. She stopped momentarily to look for her keys. Seeing it as the perfect opportunity, Mason stepped in the way.

"Kiera can you please talk to me?," Mason asked.

She looked at him with anger in her eyes. She thought of how he just walked out on him last night. She went after him, wanting to talk and he left. She had never wanted a man so much and he hurt her. He made her feel as if she wasn't good enough. She wasn't in the mood to talk. She wanted to hit him.

"What is it Mason? I have things to do," she told him. Deep down she knew she was lying.

Mason slowly walked towards her. Clenching her hands into a fists, she closed her eyes. Mason pulled her into his arms. She loved the way he smelled She wanted to hate him so much but couldn't. Suddenly she began crying.

"Baby please don't cry," Mason told her as he tried to wipe away her tears.

"What do you want Mr. Steele because I don't have time to play games. I need a man who knows what he wants," she screamed at him before shoving him away.

Mason was hurt. Her words cut like a knife. The shove away was the alcohol to the open wound. He quietly listened. She was hurting and unfortunately, he was the reason why. He knew what he wanted. He wanted her but he needed to know she was the right one for him.

"Look Kiera, I understand why you are mad at me and I am truly sorry. If you aren't too busy this weekend I was hoping we could get away from here. I want a chance to make it up to you and perhaps explain why I left," Mason said apologetically.

"Well I guess I can move some things around and make that possible," Kiera said nonchalantly. On the inside she was ecstatic.

"I really hope you can," Mason said.

"So when are trying to leave?," she asked.

"Now!," was his only response.

"Do I at least have time to run upstairs and pack a bag?," she questioned.

"Don't worry about it. We'll pick some clothes and stuff up on the way there," Mason told her as he took her hand in his.

"What? Are you serious," she asked. It shocked her and seemed so sudden.

"Kiera despite what I may have led you to believe by walking out on you last night, I really enjoyed the time we spent together. I want the opportunity to get to know you better. I was always taught not to waste time playing games when you find something you really want. I want you," he said as he stared into her eyes.

Kiera stood there frozen. She didn't want this moment to end. Did she here him right? Did he really just say he wanted her? She wanted to jump for joy. Those was the words she longed to here. She was now prepared to follow him to the ends of the earth.

Meanwhile, unknown to them they were being watched. Tre stood in Kiera's bedroom watching them through the Venetian blinds. Tre didn't like what he saw. He looked as they walked arm in arm to his car. Now that he found her, he wasn't going to lose her again. Shutting the blinds he took out his cell phone and made a call.

Vaughn sat in the car downstairs. Suddenly his phone rang. He looked at it. It was Tre calling.

"Hey boss, what's up?," Vaughn asked.

"I need you to follow them and call me as soon as they stop," Tre ordered.

"Yes boss. Do you want me to call Chameleon?," Vaughn questioned.

"Don't worry about him. Follow them like I asked and get back to me as soon as possible," Tre replied.

Vaughn started his engine and waited. Shortly after a car pulled out the lot. Sitting back in his seat, Vaughn saw Mason and Kiera inside. He waited until they were a few cars away and then pulled out behind them.

Traffic was light. They were in Long Island in a matter of minutes. Mason pulled in the mall's parking lot. They never saw Vaughn pull in behind them.

Mason ran around to Kiera's side and opened the door. Taking his hand she stepped out of the car. Closing the door, they walked inside mall. The mall was crowded. They walked into a women's clothing store. Kiera found some beautiful dresses. She went to the back and tried it on. Mason bought them all.

After that, they went and purchased some clothes for Mason. Kiera enjoyed watching him try on clothes. They laughed and talked the whole time. They even went and got some underclothes.

Suddenly their stomachs started growling. They were hungry. They decided to stop by the car and dropped off their bags. Vaughn had been waiting so long that he fell asleep.

Once they made sure the car doors were locked, they ran over to the diner across the street. They were seated near the window. All eyes seem to be on them. Kiera loved the fact, that Mason's attention was completely on her.

Kiera sat down and scooted into the booth. Mason sat down behind her. Mason held her hand. They sat laughing and talking. Shortly after, the waitress came over with the menu.

Vaughn woke up and looked around. It took him a few minutes to remember where he was. He then spotted the car. He was happy they didn't leave while he was sleep. He immediately called Tre. The phone started ringing.

"Talk to me!," Tre exclaimed.

"Hey T-rex, It's me Vaughn. I followed them out here to Long Island. Right now, we're out here at the mall. It's near a quaint little diner," Vaughn told him.
.
" Yeah, I know the place," Tre told him.

Vaughn stepped out of the car to stretch. He looked towards Mason's car and noticed the bags. "When did they come out?," he thought to himself. He looked around.

"They're in the diner," Vaughn said

"Well go inside and watch them. If they leave follow them. Keep me updated to your whereabouts. I am stuck in traffic but I'm on my way," Tre instructed him.

Vaughn turned his engine off and headed towards the diner. He could see Mason and Kiera from the outside. He studied both of them before walking in. Kiera was beautiful. He could understand why T-rex was so interested in her. Mason was a well built man and according to the information gathered on him, he was even more dangerous.

Mason watched as the stranger walked in. The man sat across from him. Something about him didn't sit well with Mason. He watched as the man would race his occasionally look their way. Finishing their food Mason went to the counter to pay the bill. His eyes traveled back and forth between Kiera and the stranger. Kiera watched him and smiled. He was so handsome.

Suddenly she saw his attention shift. She followed his gaze until she caught sight of the man Mason was watching. He seemed familiar. She needed to warn Mason. She walked up to Mason nonchalantly. She didn't want to let the man know anything was up. She held Mason's hand. The moment he looked into her eyes he knew.

133

"What is it baby?", Mason asked as he whispered in her ear.

"You see the man over there?," she questioned as she motioned in the man's direction.

"Yeah, I've been watching him. Something doesn't seem right," he told her.

"So I've noticed. Baby I'm not sure how much you remember about the night in the alley but I think he was there," she said to him.

"What? Are you sure?," he questioned trying to hide his concern.

"I am almost certain that he was the man that snuck up behind you and hit you over the head," she told him and continued. "What is he doing here? "

" I don't know," Mason said as he watched the man out of the corner of his eye. Mason had a feeling that this was no coincidence. This man was following him but why? He knew he had to get out of there. He didn't want anyone to harm Kiera. Taking her hand Kiera headed for the door. Vaughn waited a few before he headed out the door.

The manager ran behind him to remind him of his bill. Pulling money out his pocket Vaughn slammed it down on the corner and headed for the door. Mason's car was gone. Vaughn ran to his car. He couldn't believe they had gotten away. Picking up the phone he called Tre. The phone went to voicemail. He was just about to call again when suddenly, his phone rang.

"Hello," Vaughn said.

"Yeah you called. What's wrong?, " Tre asked.

"I lost them boss. I'm sorry," Vaughn said apologizing. "It's okay. After they pulled off, I went over to Mr. Steele's apartment. I believe I know exactly where they're going. Meet me there," Tre said giving Vaughn the address before hanging up.

Chapter 25

Mason did his best not to scare Kiera. He pulled out of the mall's parking lot and turned left. He looked in his rear view mirror. The coast was clear.

"Mason do you think he was following us?," Kiera asked. He could see the fear in her eyes.

"Baby I don't think he was following us. Him being in that diner may merely be a coincidence," Mason told her. He didn't exactly believe his own words.

"Mason are you sure he isn't following us?," she asked nervously.

"I'm certain. Just look around. No one is following us," he said as he reached for her hand.

Kiera was sitting low in the seat. Her hands were shaking. Her skin felt cold and clammy to the touch. Her head was immediately filled with thoughts of seeing Marcus at Geraldo's. She couldn't help but wonder if somehow they had found her. Kiera was terrified but something about Mason's touch seemed to relax her. She looked around. Seeing nothing behind them she sat up.

"Please put on your seat belt on Kiera," Mason demanded. She reached over and tugged at her seat belt. Once it was secure she glanced out the window. Trees lined the road. The scenery was breathtaking.

"Where are we going?," Kiera asked.

"You'll see in a few minutes but I want it to be a
surprise. Can I get you to close your eyes?," Mason replied
smiling.

"Really? You want me to close my eyes?," Kiera asked
laughing.

"Yes young lady. If you don't close your eyes I will
turn this car around," Mason told her jokingly.

"Yes dad," she answered playfully yet sarcastically.

Kiera closed her eyes. She could smell the flowers and
trees in the air. She listened to the sounds of the birds
calling to each other. Although she couldn't see, she was
enjoy the drive.

Mason watched her and smiled. She fell asleep after
only a few minutes. She looked so peaceful. He could watch
her every day of his life. Mason's mind played back the
day's events. He wondered if the man in the diner actually
was following him. If so why? He also wondered why Kiera
looked so frightened. Who was after her and what wasn't she
telling him.

Mason passed the old firehouse and turned right. He was
no longer near the trees. He could smell the water in the
air. Sea gulls flew overhead. He thought back to the
countless nights that he would walk to the beach, drink and
watch the rolling and crashing of the waves. He was almost
home.

Mason hadn't been there in years. It was a place filled
with bad memories. It was his constant reminder to
everything he had lost. Today he hoped it would be a new
beginning.

Ten minutes later, they pulled up in front of a
beautiful house. It was huge. A swing sat on the front
porch. There were bay windows everywhere. The lawn was well
taken care of. The grass a rich green color. There was also
a bush on lining both sides of the walkway and a tree on the
side of the house.

Mason looked over at Kiera. She still had her head back. He almost hated to wake her. He watched as the wind blowing through the window danced in her hair. Gently he brushed it behind her ear. She moaned.

"Kiera baby wake up," Mason said leaning over and whispering in her ear.

"Hmmm," she murmured and turned her head away from him.

"Baby we're here. Wake up," Mason said this time squeezing her thigh.

Kiera smiled. She stretched as she slowly woke up. Through squinted eyes she looked out the window. The confused look and indication she didn't know where here was.
 Mason backed the car into the driveway. He then got out and unlocked the doors. He then came back and grabbed the bags. Kiera watched. She was still unsure of where they were.

"Are you coming in?," Mason asked as he stood at the top of the stairs that led to the house.

"Where are we? Is this where your parents live? I was hoping to have you all to myself this weekend," Kiera inquired.

"Oh trust, there will nobody here but us this weekend," Mason said as he slowly walked down the stairs.

"Are you coming to carry me inside too?," she asked flirtatiously.

"I will if you insist," he remarked.

Mason walked over to her side and opened the door. Kiera seemed shocked. He bent down and unfastened her seatbelt. Sliding one hand under her legs and the other behind her, Mason picked her up.

Kiera immediately started giggling. She never had a man treat her this way. She stared into his eyes. She loved his romantic spirit.

"Are you serious? I do hope you know I was joking?,"
Kiera asked.

"Well I wasn't," Mason replied as pushed the car door
closed. Kiera wrapped her arms around him. Lying her head on
his chest she smiled. Mason smelled divine. No man had ever
made her feel this way.

Mason carried her up the steps with ease. Once they
reached the top he pushed the door open with his foot and carried her
over the threshold. Kiera felt like a blushing bride. She only wished Mason
was her husband.

Once inside, Mason placed her down on her feet. As he
turned to lock the door, Kiera looked around. The house was
huge. Each room was beautifully furnished. Mason stood back
and watched as she explored the whole place. He couldn't
help thinking of how much better his life would be with her in it.

"So do you think that you can tell me whose house this is
Mr. Steele?," she asked as she leaned against the kitchen
counter.

"Well Ms. Williams, it's not my parents home. They live in
Gilbert, Arizona. This is my house," he told her. She stood
there in awe. She couldn't help but wonder if he had such a
beautiful home, why he was living in the city.

She looked to find Mason searching through the cabinets.
Her stomach started growling. She was famished. "What are
you making? I'm starving. Do you need any help?," she asked
as she went back to touring the house.

"No please enjoy yourself. Let me put a little something
special together. I'll only be a little bit so please make yourself
at home," Mason said as he ushered her out of the room.
Kiera walked around once more. She passed a room she
hadn't notice before.

She walked in and noticed swords hanging on the wall. A beautiful thick white carpet in the middle of the floor. There was a fireplace as well. A desk sat in the corner and a beautiful chaise sat against the wall. She turned around and noticed a cabinet filled with medals and a uniform. She saw a photo of Mason and his unit. She studied it hard. She saw another familiar face. Was she dreaming? She couldn't believe what she was seeing. Tears welled up in her eyes. She began crying uncontrollably.

"Kiera love," Mason called out for her.

"Yes dear," she answered as she wiped the tears away with her hands.

"Time to eat sweetie," he screamed out.

"One second baby," she answered as she searched for the bathroom.

Kiera walked into the bathroom and turned on the lights. The bathroom was huge. There was a double sink with a large mirror. Music played from speakers in the wall. A Jacuzzi tub was against the wall. As she stepped further into the room, she noticed a separate room. Inside she saw the toilet and a glass shower with a place to sit down inside of it. She also saw a cabinet. Opening it, she grabbed a washcloth and went to wash her hands. She then wiped off the sink and turned off the lights.

Stepping back in the den she caught a glimpse of something lying on the floor. She walked over and was shocked with what she saw. She picked up and stuffed it into her pocket.

Kiera stepped out of the den and back into the hallway. She could hear footsteps walking towards her. Seconds later she was looking into Mason's eyes. He lit up the moment he saw her.

"Hey beautiful, I was just coming to find you," Mason said.

"Sorry you have such a beautiful home and I kind of got lost in how big it is. I did notice you have three bedrooms. Where can I place my stuff?," Kiera said.

"Don't worry your pretty self about that right now. I know that we were out shopping and only got a small bite at the diner so I made us something to eat," Mason responded.

Mason took her by the hand and led her to the kitchen. The smell of the food filled the air. Kiera's stomach growled in approval of the scent. She looked towards the table but only saw a basket. Mason grabbed the basket and walked toward the back door.

Kiera followed somewhat confused. He opened the car door and placed the basket in the back seat. Kiera stood watching.

"Am I going to have to come up there and carry you down the stairs?," Mason asked.

"No Mason. I was simply wondering where we were going?," she questioned in response.

"I want to watch the sun set with an amazingly beautiful woman over dinner," he replied.

Mason Steele was a highly decorated Army Officer. After the death of his former friend and soldier, his life took a turn for the worse. At his brink, his closest friend comes to the rescue. Now maybe he could have a second chance at life now that he has met Kiera. Unfortunately someone wants to not only destroy but kill him. Kiera seems to be running from her own horrible past. Will love triumph or will they both be destroyed???

"Where had this man been all her life? Was he just feeding her a line until he got her in bed or was this man for real?, " Both these questions_ ran through her mind. She hoped this wasn't some crazy dream. Kiera walked down the stairs. As usual Mason held the car door open for her.

Once inside, she leaned across and opened his door. Mason got in, shut the door behind him and put on his seatbelt, while he waited for Kiera to put on hers. He looked at her before putting the key in. The engine roared back to life. Mason allowed a car to pass before pulling out the driveway. He drove only a few minutes before they were back at the beach.

When he finally pulled into a parking space Kiera was staring at him. "What love?," he asked looking into her eyes.

"You have a beautiful home and are such a wonderful gentleman. To be honest it's quite refreshing. So why do you live in the city?," she answered.

"That house held too many bad memories. Being there was slowly killing me. Like I said before I want something real Kiera," he said staring into her eyes again.

He then shut the car off and hopped out to open her door. Taking her hand he helped her out the car. He then reached in the back and grabbed the basket. Mason closed her door and then took her hand. The beach was empty. Once he found a good spot he set up everything, making sure to spread the blanket out first.

Kiera stood looking impressed. Once they were seated Mason pulled out the food. He had prepared fried chicken, corn, rice and potato salad. He also had made a delicious fruit salad. Last but not least Mason pulled out some juice boxes.

"Juice boxes," Kiera said laughing.

"Last night I realized you aren't much of a drinker so, I wanted to play it safe," he replied with a smile.

Kiera shook her head. She was definitely falling fast for Mason. He was kind, attentive, intelligent, attractive and sexy. He also had a weird but adorable sense of humor. She could tell this was no act. Knowing that is what made him sexy to her. She wanted him. Mason took out the paper plates, bowls and plastic cutlery. He made Kiera's plate and then his. He handed Kiera her plate and noticed she was in a trance. He loved the fact that she was staring at him.

"Ahem!," Mason said clearing his throat and watching her.

"What?," Kiera asked once she noticed he was looking at her.

"Just breathing in your beauty and wondering what was on your mind?, Mason said to her.

"Thank you Mr. Steele," Kiera said smiling. She knew that by calling him that she could change the subject.

"Great try Ms. Williams. Now are you going to tell me what you was thinking about?," Mason continued to inquire.

"Not yet Mason. I give you my word that when the time is right, I will tell you," she vowed.

Mason was eager to know but agreed to wait. They sat, laughed and ate. They finished just before the sun began to set. The mood was perfect. Mason pulled her into his arms and kissed her. Kiera wrapped her arms around his neck. Lifting her to her feet they started dancing. The waves crashed in the background. The stars began dancing upon the quiet moonlit sea. The time seemed to fly by.

Kiera began to shiver in Mason's arms. They could feel the cold breeze coming off the water. They were so wrapped up in each other that they didn't want to leave. Suddenly it started to rain. Mason scooped the trash and placed the leftover food in the basket. When he looked at Kiera she was drenched. Her blouse clung to her breasts. Her hair was so wet it started to curl.

Even soaking wet, she was beautiful. Mason stood up and placed her hair behind her ears. Kiera stepped closer. Mason grabbed the blanket and placed it over her head.

Maybe it was the moment or the way she looked at him or maybe both, but, Mason couldn't resist any longer. He pulled her closer as he leaned in and kissed her. There tongues explored each other's mouth. Kiera moaned as he touched the small of her back.

They were so caught up in one another that they didn't notice the sound of thunder and lightning cutting the night air. They were completely soaked. They looked at each other and raced for the car. Reaching in the back seat Mason found two towels and placed them over the front seats. Kiera immediately jumped in. She was soaked from head to toe. Her nipples pressed against the drenched material. She started to shiver.

Mason turned the car on and turned up the heat. He could hear Kiera's teeth chattering. She was freezing. Reaching over her, Mason adjusted the vents. After a few minutes she began to warm up.

The rain began to come down even heavier. Mason turned on his wipers. They served little purpose. As he drove down the road, he could barely see the lines in the road. He was forced to reduce his speed to a crawl and turn on his high beams.

Chapter 26

Traffic was at a standstill. A drive that took five minutes was taking an hour. Another car was being pulled over by a police officer. Almost instantly, the traffic picked up once they drove past.

Mason shook his head. Some things never change. As long as he lived in New York, traffic always slowed down when the police pulled someone else over. Maybe it was because the other drivers were being nosey or maybe they thought the police were going to chase them. Either way it never changes.

A few minutes later they arrived back at the house. Mason backed carefully into the backyard. Once he was parked, he ran up the steps, unlocked the door and grabbed a jacket and umbrella for Kiera. He then ran down the steps and opened her door.

Kiera sat in shock. Most of the men from her past would've unlocked the house door and went to sit down leaving her to fend for herself. Once she would of made it inside they would've wanted her to cook, bring them a drink and have sex. Mason continued to amaze her.

Before stepping out the car, Kiera slipped on Mason's burgundy windbreaker jacket. Mason opened the umbrella and waited for her to step out. Once she had gotten out he handed her the umbrella. Kiera stood there waiting as he reached for the basket.

"Baby why are you still standing there?," Mason asked.

"I'm waiting for you," she quickly answered.

"I'm fine love. Go inside and get yourself warmed up. If you need a drink it's behind the bar," he told her.

Kiera looked at him and smiled. "Where had this man been all her life?" For once she felt respected and cared for. She leaned over and kissed him. He stood looking confused. Kiera turned and walked inside. Mason followed shortly after.

Once inside, they took off their shoes and socks. The whistling of the tea kettle filled the air. Mason excused himself and disappeared into the kitchen. He reemerged minutes later with two tea cups in hand. He handed one to Kiera.

"What's this?," Kiera asked.

"A little something my grandmother would make to keep us from catching cold. It's called a "Hot Toddy", Mason told her as sipped from his cup.

"Wow what a surprise. Who taught you how to make one?," Kiera questioned.

"My grandmother is from the south and would make them for my grandfather whenever he caught a cold," he said.

Kiera took a sip. It instantly warmed her up. She loved how smooth it was. She found herself getting a little sleepy. "Mason would you mind if I called it a night. This drink is making be a bit tired," she said as she excused herself.

"No not at all. I'm going to go into the kitchen and straighten it up. After that, I plan on going to bed myself," Mason replied.

Kiera turned and walked up the stairs. When she looked back Mason seemed to have vanish. She could hear the faucet running and music playing in the kitchen. She smiled at the thought of him standing over the sink shirtless.

She only stood there for a few. The feeling of wet
clothes clinging to her body was starting to irritate her.
She went through the bags they had and picked out a sexy
silk nightie and robe, her shampoo, body wash, toothbrush,
tooth paste and flat iron. The bathroom that was attached to
the room, was even bigger than the one downstairs.

There was a huge vanity mirror that covered the wall
over the double sink. The counters were made of beautiful
marble. Big fluffy towels hung on the rack. She couldn't
help but think about how different of life would be here
with Mason.

Kiera stripped out of her damp clothes. She then walked
over to the sink and brushed her teeth. When she finished
she wiped off the sink and plugged in her flat iron. While
it warmed up Kiera turned on the shower.

The water came out steaming hot. It was just the way
she liked it. The water seemed to soothe her aching muscles.
As the water streamed down her body, she imagined Mason's
fingers sliding over her flesh. She loved how comfortable it
made her feel. She could've stayed in there forever but knew
she shouldn't.

Moments later, she stepped out the tub and turned the
shower off. She reached for a towel and dried off her body.
The second towel she used to wrap up her damp hair. She then
opened the cabinet to find a jar of cocoa butter. Once she
found it she rubbed some all over her body.

Steam from the shower had fogged up the mirror. Kiera
opened the bathroom door to help clear it up. She then
reached for her nightie and robe. She slipped it on. The
material was soft and felt like a sheer layer of skin.

As she wrapped the robe around her, she slowly was able
to make out images in the mirror. She was able to see the
bed and window. Lighting flashed and she saw the peach tree
outside. Kiera began flat ironing her hair until it was nice
and straight. She quickly unplugged her flatiron and started
straightening the bathroom.

She reached for the light switch on the wall near the vanity mirror. Suddenly the lightening flashed again. She saw something moving in the tree outside. Someone was watching her. She let out a loud scream.

Mason was just stepping out the shower. His room was just down the hall. Hearing her scream, he grabbed a towel and wrapped it around him. He then reached under his pillow and grabbed his gun. Once he was certain it was loaded, Mason opened his door and raced down the hallway.

Kiera was frantic. Her skin was flushed. She pointed towards her room. Mason indicated that she should stay behind him. He then slowly walked to the room.

Kiera had left the door open. He searched in the closet and under the bed but saw nothing. He then searched the bathroom but came up empty. He looked in Kiera's direction, she was still shaking uncontrollably.

"What is it Kiera? What happened?," Mason asked almost shouting.

She pointed to the window. Mason ran to it quickly. He didn't see anything. He then ran down the hallway. He bounded down the stairs two at a time.

He looked through the peephole in the front door. He didn't see anything suspicious. Making sure the safety was off his gun, Mason pressed his body flush against the wall and opened the door. He waited a few seconds before he peeked outside.

Seeing nothing he stepped onto the porch. The swing was creaking. The wind pushed it like a father swinging his invisible child. Mason pressed his body against the house and looked down the sides. He walked down the stairs and strategically searched around and under the car. Still nothing.

Mason looked towards the house. All the lights seemed to be on. He could see Kiera nervously following his movements from inside. For the first time in a long time, he was scared. He had no idea what he would do if something happened to her.

Finally he reached the gate that led to the backyard. He carefully swung it open. The motion sensor light quickly turned on. Mason looked in the crawl space under the house.

Seeing no movement he stood back on his feet. He dust himself off. He had completely forgotten that he only had a towel on. The rain was still coming down heavy. Not only was the rain making hard to see but his towel was soaked and being weighed down.

Mason checked to make sure the towel was tightly secured around his waist. Mud and leaves now adorned it. He knew he would need another shower when he went back inside. Shrugging his shoulders he began walking to the other side of the house.

This side of the house was dark. He made a mental note to replace the bulb tomorrow. Using the house as a guide he carefully maneuvered around. The tree stood directly in front of him. Suddenly, he heard branches cracking. He whirled around. He saw two yellow eyes jumping towards him. Mason stumbled back with his gun raised.

"Meooow," it screeched at him.

Mason moved out the way. He watched as it landed and looked back at him before it ran off. Mason had to laugh at himself. He couldn't stand cats.

Mason continued walking towards the front. He diligently looked around. He didn't want to get taken off guard again. Once he reached the front, he climbed the steps.

Mason scanned the area one last time. He looked towards the lot across the street. A new house was being built. Construction equipment, steel beams and lumber lie everywhere. The tarp was only on a few of them. The rest of the tarps were blown away by the unrelenting wind.

Satisfied that nothing moved, Mason wiped his feet on the welcome mat and went inside. He locked the doors behind him and then made sure all the windows were locked.

Mason put the security code on and went to find Kiera. He found her in the living room. She was sitting on one end of the sofa, rocking back and forth and clutching the butcher's knife. Something had her terrified.

Mason approached her slowly. She stopped rocking. Her eyes locked onto Mason's. He stood there caressing her face. A solitary tear fell from her eye.

Forgetting that he still had the gun, he placed the safety on and placed it on the coffee table. They never stopped looking at one another. Mason then knelt down in front of her. He slowly eased the knife out of her hand and placed it on the table. He then pulled her close and held her.

"Baby please tell me what's wrong?," Mason pleaded.

"My ex husband is a powerful man. He has connections everywhere. He always told me if I ever left him, he would find me. Last night, when we were in the club I thought I saw one of his friends," she tearfully informed him.

"Why didn't you say anything?," he asked.

"When you showed up, I looked around and didn't see anyone so I thought I was imagining it. Then the guy at the diner got me spooked," she told him.

"I think the run in with the guy in the diner was mere coincidence. As for outside, I checked everywhere and only saw a mangy stray cat," Mason told her.

"Yeah I saw it jump out at you. Poor thing almost used up one of his nine lives," she said cracking a smile.

"Do you mind if I ask exactly who your ex husband is?," he asked.

"Can we talk about that some other time. This whole thing has scared me and left me completely drained. I just want to go upstairs and lay down," she quickly replied.

"Well you'll sleep in my room tonight. I want you to know I'll do whatever I have to in order to keep you safe," he said reassuringly.

Hearing that made her body relax. She wanted to believe him. She needed to believe him. Kiera stood up on her feet. Without saying a word, Mason scooped her up. He carefully carried her into the bedroom. He placed her on the bed and ran back downstairs to put away the knife and retrieve his gun.

When he got back upstairs Kiera had poured herself another drink. He walked in and kissed her on her lips. She smiled. Mason then excused himself as he went to take another shower. He made sure to leave the door open just in case, Kiera needed him.

A few minutes later Mason came back out of the bathroom. He was wearing a thin navy blue pair of pajama pants and no shirt. Kiera was already under the covers. Her robe now hung from the hook on the back of the bedroom door.

Mason did something that he hadn't done in a long time. He prayed. He didn't pray for himself but for Kiera. She thanked him as he stood back on his feet.

He pulled back the covers and slipped in. His body brushed against Kiera. He felt his manhood springing to life. Mason quickly slid back to give himself some room.

"Do you mind holding me? I'm still a bit shaken up," Kiera said to him.

Mason moved in closer. He wrapped his arms around her. Kiera smiled. For some reason whenever he held her she felt safe.

"Mason you seem like an amazing guy so why are you single?," she yearned to know.

"Well...," Mason said exhaling before he continued, "I have had my share of women who used me for money or sex. After my wife left me, I was broken. To be honest even the day I saw you in the window I contemplated suicide. If it wasn't for Johnny and his wife I probably wouldn't be here now.

"I'm so glad you didn't succeed," she said in awe.

"I'm glad I didn't either. Which reminds me, I owe you an explanation for last night. The first thing I want you to know is that was one of the hardest things I ever had to do," he admitted to her.

"Why do you say that?," Kiera asked laughing to herself.

"Kiera you are a true vision of undeniable beauty. I am just at the point where I want something more. I need someone real. I am so tired of coming home to an empty life. I want love. I want a wife and some kids of my own," he said. Tears started to fall from his eyes.

Kiera wiped the tears away. She then looked Mason in the eye. He was the man she had always prayed for. She couldn't believe he was finally hers.

"Let me love you Mason," Kiera pleaded.

"Only if you are willing to trust me and allow me to love you in return" Mason said.

Sitting up, Kiera looked into his eyes. She could see that he meant what he said. This amazing man was asking her if he could love her. She soon found herself crying.

Mason kissed her tears away and brushed her hair. Kiera wrapped her arms around him. Leaning in he kissed her. She moaned in response. Their breathing was getting hot and heavy. Kiera kicked the sheets off of her. She was naked. Mason stopped. He wanted her. His body was aching with passion. He needed to know if this was going to be something more.

"Kiera baby," he said as she kissed his neck.

"Mason I want you to make love to me," she begged.

"Believe me when I tell you Kiera, there is definitely a fire burning inside of me. I would love nothing more than to make love to you but I need something more," he said. Hearing the words escape his mouth even surprised him.

No man had ever turned her down. Here they were and her body hungered for him. She knew she wanted more than a moment with him. She wanted forever.

"Mason believe me it is shocking to hear but you are the first man I've ever met who wanted what's in my heart. Although, I feel a little rejected I actually desire you more. I have always wanted a man that can love me for me," she said smiling.

"I am glad to hear that love. I want a wife and a soulmate and if we are meant to be, when the time is I give you my word, I will do things to you that will make your body shiver. I will make you not only bite your lip but speak in tongues. On that day I will devour and make love to every inch of your body. You will know that you finally have a man that truly loves you," he vowed to her.

Kiera knew her heart had finally found the man she was meant to be with. Mason was her soulmate. He was her today, tomorrow and always. She was willing to wait because she was already in love with him.

Kiera got up and reached for her robe. Putting it on she climbed back in bed. Mason looked at her and smiled. She could see something in his eyes. Something deep. For the first time in her life she knew she had found a man who she could share her dreams and her darkest secrets with. Mason was a man she could spend her life with.

"Can I lay here in your arms?," she asked.

"Of course my love. I would spend forever holding you close and getting lost in the beauty of your eyes," he said as he wrapped his arms around her. Soon after they fell asleep.

Chapter 27

Mason woke up the next morning. He reached for Kiera. She wasn't there. The smell of a well cooked breakfast filled the air. Swinging his feet off the side of the bed, Mason headed towards the kitchen.

As soon as Mason got downstairs he was greeted by an amazing sight. Kiera stood next to the stove making pancakes. She was whining her hips to some reggae music. He stood there for a few just watching.

Kiera turned around smiling. She was surprised to see him standing there. She was so into the music, that she never heard him coming. Putting down the bowl, Kiera rushed into his arms.

"Hey handsome, how did you sleep?," she asked.

"Fine baby," he said as he pulled Kiera closer and kissing her.

She loved how his lips felt against hers. Kiera closed her eyes and wrapped her arms behind his head. His tongue explored her mouth. She never wanted it to end but, broke the kiss.

"Whoa daddy, you're going to have to slow down. You can't keep teasing a girl and then making her wait. Come sit down. As soon as I finish making breakfast, you can eat," Kiera told him.

Kiera then turned and walked into the kitchen. Mason walked closely behind her. He licked his lips and smiled. Just as soon as she took the bowl back into her hands, Mason reached out and pinched her butt.

She let out a loud scream and placed the bowl back down. Whirling around she looked at Mason. He sat pretending not to know what happened. She gently spanked the back of his hand with hers and smiled.

"Are you going to let me finish making this breakfast or am going to have to make you sit in a corner and face the wall?," she asked sarcastically.

"Okay mommy, I'll behave. Scouts honor," Mason replied playfully as he crossed his fingers behind his back.

"Tell me something Mason were you ever even a boy scout?," she questioned. Her hand were on her hips.

"Honestly no Kiera," he confessed.

"You are too much," she said.

"Better too much than too little baby," he replied.

"You don't have any reason to worry about that," she mumbled under her breath. She then turned and went back to cooking.

A few minutes later Kiera was done. The food was incredible. They sat back just eating and talking. Mason had never enjoyed himself with anyone the way he was now. Suddenly, Mason's cellphone rang. Kiera picked the phone up off the counter and passed it to him.

"Hello!," he said answering the phone.

Johnny was on the other end. Apparently he needed me. He had just received a call from Police Detective Calloway of the Homicide Unit. He said it was very important so Mason agreed to be there in two hours. Satisfied with that, they hung up the phone.

"Sorry Kiera but Johnny needs me in the office. Would you be okay coming with me?," Mason said as he turned and looked at her.

"If it's okay I would rather stay here and straighten up," she answered.

"Are you sure baby? After last night I would feel more comfortable if you were with me," he told her.

"I am sure I'll be fine," she said confidently.

"Alright, I'll leave my back up weapon in the hallway desk just in case, of an emergency.

Mason then rushed upstairs to shower. Kiera offered to iron his clothes just to save him some time. After ten minutes, he was ready. Kiera walked him outside to the car.

"You sure that you'll be alright?," Mason inquired.

"I promise I will fine baby", she replied.

"Okay well, make sure to lock the door behind me. I place the gun in the desk. Call me if you need anything," he told her.

"Yes dad," Kiera said.

Kiera gave him a long juicy wet kiss. Mason hated to leave but had to get to the office. He revved up his engine and pulled out the driveway. He honked his horn and then drove off.

Kiera stood there watching him drop off. She couldn't help but imagine how it would feel if he was her husband. She imagined him drive off to work and coming home to her everyday.

When she couldn't see him any more, she turned to go back inside. She locked the door behind her. Music resonated from the kitchen. Feeling the beat Kiera began dancing.

Suddenly, there was a knock on the front door. Kiera looked through the peephole. It was Mason. "Maybe he forgot something or missed me," she thought to herself.

She unlocked the bolt lock on the door. Slowly she began turning the knob. She stopped. Something was wrong. "He should have a key so, why is he knocking", she said to herself.

 She attempted to lock the door back. BOOM! The door shattered apart. Splinters of wood went flying everywhere. Kiera stumbled back as she fell to the ground. She was now face to face with the man she believed was Mason.

    "Who are you?," she asked back peddling as she tried to get to the gun.

    "Is that anyway to treat me?," the doppelganger asked her.

    The voice sounded horrifyingly familiar. She shook her. She couldn't believe it was him. The last time she saw him, he was scratching at his face after she'd thrown bleach at him. He ripped off his mask. Looking at her he started laughing. Kiera looked back at the table. She had to keep stalling.

    "Remember me now?," he asked as he began to close the distance between them.

    "Cameron," she said. The name made her tremble in fear just saying it.

    "Is that any way to act Kiera?," he questioned.

    She kept moving backwards. She could feel the edge of the rug. She knew she was close. She started smiling.

    "So you want the proper welcome you deserve?," she asked him, seconds from the gun.

    "That would be nice. How about a little kiss?," he asked. She could see his teeth through his badly damaged skin as he smiled.

    She was terrified. He now looked like the monster he had become. "Just a few more inches," she thought to herself. Suddenly she banged against something huge.

"Hi honey! I'm home," a voice said from behind her.

Kiera whirled around. She was now face to face with her living nightmare. Her ex husband Tre stood over her. Fear now completely washed over her. She reached for the drawer. Pulling it open she grasped the gun in her. Thankful that Mason showed her how to use it before he had left, Kiera took it off safety and prepared to shoot. With lightning fast speed Tre grabbed the gun and hit Kiera. She crumbled onto the ground motionless.

Chameleon immediately ordered his men into the house. He walked around with a disgusted look on his face. He walked into the den. He studied the pictures on the wall.

Without warning he began tearing everything off the wall. In his mind Mason should be dead. He didn't want Mason to live happily ever after like the fairy tales. He wanted to watch him suffer. Once he and him alone decided Mason had suffered enough, he wanted him lying dead at his feet.

"Grab everything that looks important," he ordered.

"What about her boss?," Vaughn asked as he walked past.

"Put her in the van. She's going with us and put a guard on her. If she tries anything kill her," Chameleon ordered, totally disregarding Tre.

Excerpt From

Unmasked : "The True Face Of A Monster"

   Kiera slowly stirred awake. Her face felt as if she had
ran into a truck. Vibrations traveled up and down her spine.
She felt the cold steel against her face.

   She could hear the tires as they hit a bump. Feeling
groggy Kiera sat up and looked out the window. Mason's house
was getting smaller and smaller. They had found her. As the
house completely vanished in the distance, Kiera couldn't
help but wonder if she would ever see Mason again...

A Rising Son Publication

Made in the USA
Columbia, SC
22 April 2023

15663450R10100